I was the Lady of Shalott

A NOVELLA
Theodora Perfect

This book is dedicated to those who believe in

courtly love, and beauty in nature.

First edition

ISBN 978-1-77934-066-5

The characters in this book are entirely fictional, and have no connection whatsoever with any individuals past or present.

I was the Lady of Shalott

Lucy sat in front of the mirror of her dressing table in a dressing gown and pyjamas brushing her hair while she ran through in her mind all the items she had to deal with before the wedding. Taped to her mirror was a wedding invitation. Her older stepbrother, Michael, who worked for the British Council in Kolkata, was getting married to his long-term girlfriend, and Lucy was to be a bridesmaid. She peered at her face, drew down her eyebrows into a deep frown like a Chinese dragon, pursed her lips, tentatively tugged at a few wayward hairs in one eyebrow. Her skin was smooth with no blemishes. She saw no need for make-up.

She was very proud of her hair which grew straight and thick and had been likened to sun-dried wheat by a secret admirer at school. When brushed out and allowed to hang naturally it reached her shoulders. Starting at her temples, with head tilted to one side, she tugged her hairbrush vigorously through the heavy coils with short sharp movements, first one side then the other. It always had a profound calming effect on her mood; like stroking a cat. When her hair began to glow and the static crackle, she grasped it tightly with the other hand and wrapped an elastic hair grip around it drawing it away from the nape of her neck at the same time. She had an appointment to have it cut later that day in the village. From her selection of baseball caps she chose her favourite one. It was emerald green with a stallion embroidered on the front. She put it on and pulled her ponytail through the back.

The only dresses Lucy had ever worn were at school. She felt most comfortable in jeans or calf-length shorts in summer. The thought of having to wear a dress for the wedding filled her with dread. That also meant high-heeled shoes. Another one of Lucy's chief hates. She owned three sets of trainers which she wore all the year round. For going out into the soggy fields she wore Wellington boots which sat in a large wooden crate near the front door and were not allowed in the house at any time. One of her mother's golden rules.

Twice a week Lucy would take her mother down to the gym in the village and spend an hour working out on the machines. Her mother would spend some time on a bicycle machine, but nothing more strenuous. Lucy had a routine she followed each time that also involved weights. After that they would sit and chat in the cafe over a coffee with several of her mother's friends. The personal trainers would come over and chat. Lucy flirted with them in a half-hearted manner. None of them had the sort of build she found attractive. They were too brawny. Too muscled. None of the parts related to the whole.

Her mother had never learnt to drive. When her father was alive this had not been a problem, but now, her mother relied on her entirely for getting around the village to do shopping and for visiting friends.

Lucy needed to pick up the dress she was to wear for the wedding and the shoes to match and various other important accessories. She studied her fingernails in turn and debated whether to have them painted and decided against it. For the heat of Kolkata, she had decided to wear sandals. Perhaps she should have her toenails painted as they would be visible? Should she have her fingernails painted at the same time? What about jewellery? So many issues to deal with! Lucy had never had her ears pierced at the time all her friends were having theirs done. It all seemed too frivolous and girlish. She was never one to follow the herd. Her very first passport that had never been opened was stowed away carefully in a drawer in her dressing table.

As she got up from her chair, she carefully skirted the farmyard scene that lay spread out on the carpet against one wall with her favourite horses in their paddocks, which all had their names on the doors of their stables. She bent down to arrange a cow that had fallen over. It had a broken leg and needed to lean against something. On one wall of her bedroom in a neat line all her pony club rosettes were proudly displayed.

Lucy made her bed. Something that had been imprinted on her by her mother from the time she was a little girl, folded her nightie neatly and placed it under the pillows, placed her old Teddy bear between them, tucked her slippers under the bed.

Every Wednesday evening a friend of her mother's would collect her mother for the weekly bridge with some of the ladies in the village. With her mother out of the house, Lucy could not be bothered to heat up the remains of the steak and kidney pie they had eaten for lunch. She would phone Charlie. Charlie was an old friend from university, and someone Lucy had invited to the wedding, much against her mother's wishes.

It suddenly occurred to her that Charlie was giving a talk somewhere. It was at the Town Hall. Lucy looked for the invitation. She found it. Town Hall, seven pm. Charlie was always good value. Eccentric. Always capable with her unconventional approach to life, she managed to make Lucy feel better, no matter what. With her car loaded with packages, Lucy decided against going home and instead, headed straight for the Town Hall.

Lucy was surprised to find the Town Hall parking lot full. It took several minutes to find a space for her short wheelbase Land Rover. As she walked up the steps of the old Victorian building, she glanced at her watch and saw she had missed most of the talk. She heaved open the heavy oak doors as quietly as possible, closing them carefully behind her. She surveyed the packed silent hall which smelled strongly of floor polish and ages of sweat. There was a vacant chair in the back row. She squeezed past the stout legs of Mrs Cooper who ran the dairy farm down the road. Mrs Cooper scowled. Lucy looked around and found she recognised most of the faces. A few looked in her direction and smiled.

Charlie's strong voice could be clearly heard from the stage. The hall was used by the local repertory company to stage concerts with music from the shows, and at Christmas the pantomime, not to mention flower shows.

'Dear ladies, to finish off with a few statistics. The average woman in her lifetime will have sex more than three thousand times. A man will have an orgasm every time he has sex. But what about the poor woman? What about her orgasm? How often does she have an orgasm? One woman in three will have difficulty having an orgasm during sex with a man.'

'Listen to this. Once a man has had his orgasm he is finished. His brain disallows any further sexual thoughts. The woman, however, can go on and have several, if not many orgasms after that. Orgasms are so good for you. They release endorphins referred to as runner's high. Endorphins are good for dispelling depression. They tone up your system. Women use up 90 calories per half hour during sex. Sex raises your heart rate to around 130 beats a minute, which is roughly the same effect as climbing stairs for 15 to 20 seconds – so if you feel comfortable climbing stairs, sex shouldn't be a heart attack issue.'

'What I am getting at here, ladies is this. We do not have to rely on a man for an orgasm. We can achieve this easily and cheaply without mess or getting pregnant or getting an STD or AIDS. With the use of a simple gadget that only costs fifty pounds, you have at your fingertips a device which can provide you with an orgasm, any time you like, in the comfort of your very own home. This is what I am referring to. This little fellow is made by Hitachi. It is the acme tool for orgasms. It is reliable and very reasonably priced.'

'Are there any questions?'

A few brave hands went up. Charlie deftly provided answers.

'That's it ladies and gentlemen. Thank you for coming along.'

The hall exploded into applause.

Lucy waited until the hall had emptied, before getting to her feet and making her way towards Charlie who had a few people clustered around her. Charlie caught sight of her and grinned broadly.

'Lucy, what an unexpected surprise.' Lucy gave Charlie a big hug.

'I wasn't sure if you knew the topic of my talk.'

'I admit I was a little taken aback when I saw it on the board outside.'

'You did seem a bit squirmy sitting there. As if you had ants in your pants.'

'I was sitting next to Mrs Cooper who supplies us with milk. Never, mind. You seemed to hit the spot. No pun intended!'

'That! It went better than I expected. Look, Lucy, I've so much I need to say to you. The wedding and all that. I've been so busy trying to make money for the airfare. The usual sort of thing when you're self-employed. Why don't we buy a pizza and take it back to my flat? We can have a chat, and I can brief you on my plans for the wedding, and you can do the same. How about that?'

'Good idea.'

'Fantastic. Let me order now so we don't have to wait ages when we get there. I know just the place. I'm a great fan of theirs. There's a really sexy little Bangladeshi waiter who always gives me the eye when I collect my order. What do you like? I usually have the Four Seasons. Another nice one is Cappriciosa – ham, mozzarella, and artichokes. Let's have a Four Seasons and share?'

'Good idea.'

Charlie called the Pizza parlour.

'Saucy devil. The Bangladeshi waiter wanted to know if I wanted anything else, in a very suggestive manner? That's done. Shall we go. Follow me MacDuff.'

'Right.'

Charlie was driving a pale blue Ford Escort which had streaks of mud along the sides. A mud flap waggled from the rear wheel. One tire bulged. It would need a service if it were to pass its next MOT.

On the way to Charlie's flat in the outskirts of the town, they passed the parlour and collected their pizzas. The Bangladeshi was busy on the phone. When he saw Charlie, he held up his thumb and winked lasciviously. They were served by a surly English girl with a nostril stud and plucked eyebrows chewing gum. They reached the row of terraced houses where Charlie rented a basement flat. They parked in a small courtyard at the back beside two pickups.

Charlie brought a large box from the boot of her car which she handed to Lucy. It smelled divine. Charlie switched on a light in the wall that illuminated a flight of narrow red-brick steps that spiralled down to the front door. A spray of jasmine dangled over the wall. The wind had blown a pyramid of dead leaves into a corner of the wall. Charlie rummaged in her large handbag for the front door key. In the process she dropped her cell phone which skidded across the wet floor.

'Bugger it.'

Lucy rescued the phone which showed signs of earlier abuse while Charlie searched for the key. At long last the key was found. Attached to it was a small fluffy tiger. Charlie opened the door and kicked aside a mountain of old newspapers and circulars that was blocking the door.

'Come along in.' Charlie started singing. "This is where the one who knows meets the one who does not care." Chris Rea. I love his lyrics. Let me take your coat. The loo is down the corridor on the left. Put that box on the table. Phew, we need to open a window.'

Along one wall hung large photographic prints of flowers that suggested parts of the female anatomy: an orchid, hibiscus, and a rose. Lucy studied them, head to one side.

A very fat ginger cat appeared at an open window. It squeezed through a gap in the curtain and hopped down onto the carpet and rubbed its cheek against Charlie's calves, meowing in a guttural voice.

'Good evening Mr. Oscar. Can you smell pizza? His full name is Oscar Wild. I found him in a cardboard box outside the supermarket. If I bring a male into this flat, he turns his back and stalks out in a huff. Don't you my dear boy? I hope that cardigan is not mohair, Lucy. Oscar has an absolute passion for mohair sleeves, don't you my darling, even though he's been done? He straddles your arm, sinks his teeth into your wrist, rubs his little crotch into the wool until he comes. Try and stop him, and he savages you with his sharp little teeth. Don't you, my boy?' Oscar started purring.

'Yes, you know I'm talking about you.' Oscar raised his tail until it pointed at the ceiling and began twitching it ecstatically.

On the opposite wall were two large, framed prints of nudes by Austrian artist Egon Schiele.

'There's someone who knew how to draw. In my opinion, he has the nicest line of any artist you can name. Maybe Picasso was more fluent. I also like the drawings by Augustus John who you don't hear much of these days. I've tried copying that one by Schiele and I had great difficulty getting the texture of the hair. It looks so simple, but it ain't. That was his sister.'

'Not very elegant!'

'But hugely erotic. At first glance they appear pornographic, even by today's standards. And yet he adored women. His father died of dementia caused by syphilis; his poor mother obviously suffered from it too because she had three babies in a row that were still born. He was the youngest student at sixteen to enter the Academy of Art in Vienna. He had a mistress who'd been a prostitute and modelled for him even at the time he married a lady who was minor gentry. He also used street kids for models. He was imprisoned for being degenerate. During the first outbreak of influenza to hit Europe, his young wife who was expecting their first baby, caught it and so did he. She died, and a week later he died. He was only twenty-eight. Really tragic.'

Charlie found plates and cutlery. 'How about a glass of wine, Lucy? I'm feeling rather thirsty after all that speechifying.'

'That would be nice.'

'I got six bottles of this Chilean wine from that new Indian takeaway that's opened opposite the Methodist church. Special Offer! Probably got smuggled in with a container load of migrants.'

Charlie poured two large glasses, spilling a little as she poured, catching the falling drops deftly with her finger and licking it.

'Cheers!' She took a long swig from her glass. 'Ooh, that tastes good. I've a theory that great art comes out of an overdeveloped libido. Look at Mozart. Bach fathered twenty children. Picasso. Nureyev.'

'Where's your masterpiece Charlie? You have the libido. What's lacking?'

'I don't have the discipline. You do. Why don't YOU do something? After all you studied English literature for your degree. Come on girl!'

'I'm waiting for inspiration. I need a bit of jogging. Just you wait!'

Charlie waited for Lucy to elaborate but she said nothing more.

The girls ate from trays on their laps. Charlie lassoed a skein of cheese that dangled from her chin with her large pink tongue reminding Lucy of a chameleon.

'Lucy, first things first. This wedding. I'm terribly broke at the moment. To find the money for the air ticket to Kolkata is pushing my limits, some. But, guess what?'

Oscar began batting a piece of crust across the carpet as though he was delivering the coup de grace to a field mouse. The crust went under the sofa and joined the other pieces of jetsam that Charlie's Jamaican cleaner could not reach with the hoover.

'You've won the lottery?'

'Not quite! Think again.'

'You've been given an illustrated version of the Egyptian book of the dead written in Sanskrit?'

'Good try. Ta Ra, out of the blue, I've won a prize for a travel article I wrote on Bangkok, given by one of the hotel chains. The prize is… just listen to this! Airfare and four nights in a luxury hotel in Bangkok for two!'

'Wow!'

'I've quite a bit of potential work waiting for me in Bangkok. I need to firm those up with the odd meeting here and there. I also have one or two ideas for articles for an erotic magazine I write for now and again. What I'm saying here, is this. It would be a great pity to waste this opportunity, not so?'

'I agree heartily. When does the offer expire?'

'Fairly soon, actually. Why don't you and I stop over for four nights in Bangkok en route to Kolkata? It's a million miles away from the mud and poo of a Somerset farmyard. You'll be bowled over. I've been there several times, know the place pretty well, speak a few words of the lingo, know a guy out there who is quite cute called Boribun. It's such an exciting place. The flight time from Bangkok to Kolkata is just over an hour. We can have fun together before the big day. Loosen up a bit. What do you think?'

'I'll think about it. There's my dear mother to consider. She's driving me crazy at the moment.'

'I know, I know.'

'Why don't I talk it over with her and phone you back tomorrow evening?'

'Right. Another glass of wine?'

'Okay.'

'Do you remember that movie we went to at university by Peter Greenaway? The Cook, the Thief, His Wife and Her Lover? It had Helen Mirren in it. Well, I've found another of his movies, The Pillow Book.'

'What's it about?'

Charlie reading from the sleeve. 'It's about a … the print on these DVDs is enough to test the eyesight of a ten-year old … young Japanese girl whose father is a skilled calligrapher. He's also trying to become a famous writer. He comes under the spell of his publisher who demands favours from him in order to get his writing published. On her birthdays her father draws on her forehead a symbol. When she grows up her passion is for a skilled calligrapher to write a book on her own naked body.'

'I like the idea of skin being used for art. A beautiful woman whose body becomes the canvas for exquisite calligraphy,' said Lucy.

'Let's look the movie up on Wiki. I want to get a small tattoo. Size is time and time is money. It'll be a tiger. At the base of my spine at the Maladahar chakra, the source of Kundalini, the divine source of feminine energy.'

'You like tigers. I see you have one on your keyring.'

'I think they're very noble creatures, and very sure of themselves. Their markings are gorgeous.'

'I agree wholeheartedly with that. What on earth's a chakra?'

'Oriental people who are way more enlightened than we are believe that chakras are points in the human body from which energy flows. Western medicine does not recognise them at all.'

'Do you seriously believe in any of this?'

'I do and I do not. In the West we're conditioned to believe everything we hear from the rational scientifically tested medical point of view. There's much more out there we know nothing about, so I tend to go for anything like this as long as it doesn't do me any harm or anybody else.' Oscar had curled up on the sofa between the two girls and was washing his paws.

Charlie continued, 'The Buddhists have a very long association with tattooing. Tattoos done by priests in the traditional manner have great power. Remember most Thais are Buddhist. That means they're very tolerant of what we consider misfits. Their belief is to show love and compassion to all sentient beings. My favourite tattoo artist is Japanese. He works freehand and does exquisite paintings in the manner of traditional Japanese art. His name is Gakkin. On one level tattoos in Japan are an indication of fellowship with a criminal gang. On the other, they are an art form. I could never afford one of his tattoos, so I will go for a simple one that is not too conspicuous. Buddhists have also developed a style of massage which is much like yoga. That is also one of the things on my wish list when we get there. The Wat Po, the Reclining Buddha monastery, is the centre for traditional Thai massage. This is performed in the monastery cloisters by students from their massage school. You need to have one. We could make the Wat Po our first point of call and follow it with a massage. I've had one and it really tones you up for the day.'

'I've always wanted to do yoga, but its finding someone who can teach it, that's the big problem living in rural England.'

Charlie continued, 'They have a holistic belief in health out there. There are strong connections between their massage and yoga, for sure. Their pressure points are the same as those used by acupuncturists. You can get a ticket at the same time as you book to go into the monastery. Be on the alert. Thai males are very promiscuous. With your gorgeous blonde hair, just you watch out. I remember a BBC programme about it. There are surgeons in Thailand who specialise in sewing on penises that have been severed by irate and desperate wives. The clever part for the spouses is making it impossible for the adulterous husband to become reconnected with his penis. Flushing it down the toilet is the most popular way, stuffing it into the food mixer is another, or throwing it out of the window of a speeding motorcar. In Thailand it has become known as "feeding the ducks." One very enterprising lady used a balloon filled with helium.'

'Come on. I don't believe any of this!'

Charlie found another bottle of wine. 'Where have I put the damn corkscrew? Ah, here it is.' She struggled a bit to get the cork out. Making her way gingerly across the carpet in Lucy's direction she stumbled over one of Oscar's fluffy toys.

'No more for me Charlie, honestly, I'm feeling tipsy already.'

'No harm in that. Come on.'

'No honestly.'

'Move over Oscar. I want to sit next to my friend. Move!' Oscar reluctantly hopped down onto the carpet. Charlie sat down heavily next to Lucy.

'Lucy tell me about your idea of true love? You've got such a yummy body. If I had half your bodily assets, I'd be a highly paid escort in Las Vegas. Do you know the top ones earn six hundred dollars an hour?'

'That is a lot! I'll let you into a little secret. Let me tell you about a little stratagem I conceived at the time when most of my friends were having affairs and losing their virginity. Chatting to these girls after the event it all seemed so petty and frequently sordid. More than half were drunk at the time and remembered little about it. I didn't want any of that. I didn't want it to be like learning to ride a bicycle or jumping out of an airplane with a parachute. I wanted it to be carefully stage-managed, like a play, with an actor I had chosen for the role, costumes that I provided, the make-up, the location. All of this, I thought about it a lot. In literature the world over virginity is a precious commodity. It has been for thousands of years. It symbolises so much. For me, at any rate!'

'You're being so serious and theatrical. Go on.'

Lucy giggled. 'I bought a small money box that I decorated on the outside with white silk. Inside I lined it with red velvet. It could be locked. After the event I was to write down in detail what it felt like and place it in the box with my knickers. At a certain date in the future I would open the box, read the account, and ask myself if deep down, I felt any different.

'And did you?'

'No.' Lucy couldn't stop giggling. 'Oh God...'

'Come on. Get a grip of yourself young lady! What do you mean, no?'

'Nothing happened.'

'What? Nothing! He couldn't get it up?'

'No, no! It was a terrible disaster from beginning to end. The Adonis I chose had a beautiful body. He was a swimmer.'

'Lucy, you old devil. What happened? Reveal all, leave no smutty detail unturned, I say. Come on!'

Oscar rolled over and started purring loudly.

'The chosen one was all I could have imagined. But once we started kissing I tasted alcohol. He smelt of booze. He became rough. So, I sent him home. I was disgusted.'

'The poor little guy must have been absolutely terrified. You said he was shy. No wonder. Fancy coming up against someone who'd prepared the whole thing like a game-plan for a rugby match. He must have been frightened shitless. I can picture him swigging back the beer while seeking advice from all his mates in the common room. Their suggestion of course was to get pissed. Typical male reaction.'

Oscar sidled up to Lucy with tail erect. She ran her fingers along his spine against the nap causing him to twitch his tail.

'Watch it. No Oscar! He sprays when he gets excited. So, you're still a virgin and the little casket lined in red remains empty. You've no idea what that little casket symbolises with its red velvet lining, do you? God Lucy! Think what Salvador Dali could have done with that. Did you know with the help of an Argentinian jeweller he constructed intricate works of art out of precious stones? Many had tiny electric motors which caused petals to open and close, and hearts to pump? Bit kitsch. Very Roman Catholic. Not that Salvador was anything of a church goer, though.'

'No. I didn't do History of Art and Architecture like you did. Wish I had though. And the cost?'

'Millions. Nobody could own a piece. They were just too valuable. Can you write down what your little stratagem was and send it to me? It will be good practice for when you get struck by inspiration and produce your major œuvre littéraire.

'Of course I will. I'll send it to you as soon as I have finished it.'

'Great. I look forward to that. What's your ideal body type?'

'I don't like body hair – beards, moustaches, hairy chests, hairy arms and so on. I like clean-shaven faces. I like swimmer's bodies that are lean and powerful for cleaving the water like dolphins. Aerodynamic like otters. Narrow hips, flat stomachs, powerful calves and thighs. Well-developed shoulders. I don't like weight-lifter's bodies – heavy and out of proportion, gross. Ears also. Michelangelo had the right idea. His David is gorgeous.'

'His David has a good head of hair though?'

'I do prefer shaved heads, I must admit. Sleek, no nonsense faces with good cheek bones. Broad foreheads. Long noses. Small ears. Fine eyebrows, nicely shaped lips with a top lip full and a bottom lip bursting like a ripe cherry. Necks are important for me. Slim and graceful. Buttocks are the most exciting part of a body to me.

Rounded, firm, well-proportioned. Narrow. Potent. Calves, round tapering down to narrow ankles. I like feet too. Nice ones, that is. Ilike feet to be neat and well cared for. Nails nicely trimmed. I don't like crooked toes. Thumbs are very important. An ugly thumb can turn me off instantly.'

'For heaven's sake, what's an ugly thumb?'

Lucy extended her right hand to illustrate her point.

'The thumb has one joint or knuckle. If the joint with the nail is small by comparison with the rest, that makes it very ugly. Each phalange should be about the same length to allow the nail part to be long and elegant. It should incline slightly upwards. It's hard to explain.'

'You've obviously given the whole matter some thought. Sex by itself? Do you get horny? Need a man, no matter what?'

'No, not really. I go for a ride on my trusted charger, who's called Blaze, if I do feel that way. I must admit galloping does stimulate me in a funny sort of way.'

'They say it's possible for a woman to have an orgasm on a horse. Never thought of it in that way. It must do something for the rider because how many little girls go through the horsey period during puberty until they find real men. Oscar Wilde believed that horses were dangerous at both ends and uncomfortable in the middle. Have you ever seen a man's penis?'

'My brother's. I've seen enough stallions's with big erections. Stallions do turn me on, I must admit. Long, thick and with those bulging heads like clenched fists. If you want to know what goes through my mind when I am fantasising about sex? It's of a gorgeous woman with flowing golden hair galloping naked on a large black horse along a beach at dawn.'

'Wow! That speaks volumes, dear girl. I have a funny feeling you may be entering an exciting phase of your life. Here you are twenty-two years of age, still a virgin, in the prime of your life when you have everything going for you, and you're without a partner. You've never experienced full on sex before. That must be some sort of record!

What goes wrong? You've a really scrummy body, nice boobs, not too big, well-shaped. Pointy nipples. A very saucy bottom, shapely legs. You've got lovely eyes, lips made for kissing. Hair to die for. I'm not a guy, so I don't know what turns them on. But for me, you have it all, and much, much more! So, tell me. Where does it all go wrong?'

Lucy frowned, sighed, and shrugged her shoulders.

'I went to a party with a school friend. We'd just finished our "O" levels. Amanda had been invited by another friend who had stacks of money and a huge house. Her friend, the one with the money, invited a few close friends, but someone sent out an open invitation on social media. Her parents were away for the whole weekend. Well, masses of older guys arrived uninvited. It was chaos. They started wrecking the place. Neighbours phoned the police. It was too dreadful. I managed to escape and got home in a taxi. I couldn't find Amanda. She woke up naked in one of the bedrooms. She felt very sore. She told her mother who took her to their doctor. She was given all sorts of stuff to avoid pregnancy. Since then, I've become very critical of guys and their motives.'

'That happens all too frequently, I'm afraid... that's how they're constructed.'

'I don't look at every relationship in those terms. As soon as I get the feeling the guy is seeking his own physical fulfilment, above all else, I freeze and want out. If the guy has not the slightest interest in what I think, or what I feel, that also produces a deep freeze in the relationship. I put a lot of store in sensations. Has the guy got an unpleasant body odour? Has he got a lot of body hair? Does he clean his teeth? Are his finger-nails clean? Any one of these can bring the shutters down. The last guy I went out with felt challenged if he was not with a bunch of other guys all the time. I could never have him all to myself. There had to be at least one other person with us wherever we went. Booze is a major turn-off for me. And smoking. A glass of wine or one or two beers fine, but when the person loses grip of who he is, that's it.'

'Lucy you're looking for someone who's not really human.

All those no-no's you've mentioned are all human characteristics which you just have to overlook if the relationship is going to succeed. They don't amount to much in the general equation. Don't you have physical cravings? Can you see the physical side of a relationship apart from the emotional?'

'No, I see it as all part and parcel of the whole. It is all the extraneous bits which go to make the whole. I think sex is such a huge event that you should be totally aware of what is going on at every moment and not have your senses dulled with wine or drugs.'

'Your knight in shining armour becomes a purely fictional creature who doesn't breathe air or eat or excrete. The more he becomes a fictional character the less you're able to appreciate that he is a human being with quirks and defects like any other human being. You're treating sex which is lodged in the old part of your brain with attitudes which arise in your evolved new brain. It's like trying to evaluate the taste of an exquisite Indian curry using a multiple-choice questionnaire. It just doesn't work.'

'No, I'm aware of all those things. If I'm patient, it'll happen, and then I'll be bowled over.'

'How often does this happen?'

'Being turned off? It happens with boring regularity. So much so, that right now I cannot find the energy to go out with a guy anymore. I just know it'll end in disaster.'

Charlie shook her head. 'So sad Lucy. So sad.'

Oscar found a crust of pizza and began batting it across the carpet.

'What about your lovers, Charlie? What do you look for in a male?'

'Me! Oh God! I take what comes along, really. If I'm really horny, I reach for the rolling pin or the ironing board or the knob on the bedstead. Like Oscar over there. When the mood takes me. The guys who find their way into my bed tend to be hairy, drunk, untidy, smelly, freckly. You know? The typical Anglo Saxon arsehole type.'

'And what was your very worst experience?'

'Oh, there was the time when I was in bed with this guy I met at a pub. We were kissing away and he suddenly sat up and puked all over my stomach.'

'Really gross! And the best?'

'No doubt the time I went climbing in the Brecon Beacons with that young guy from Sri Lanka. Remember? He had one of those unpronounceable names. Tillakaratne de Silva, if I remember rightly. He played cricket. He had the sort of body you're talking about. A working body with muscles that were right. He wrote essays for me. He wrote beautifully. I always got A's. He wanted to become a novelist. Adored Michael Ondaatje.'

Charlie tickled Oscar under his chin. 'Isn't it amazing how people for whom English is not their native tongue can write better prose than those for whom it is? He was passionate about dippers. We came on this spectacular waterfall. He spotted this dipper flitting about – a small bird that likes swimming in fast-flowing streams. He fell in and was thrashing about as though he was drowning. I went in after him and it turned out he was only messing about. He pulled me into the water. It was one of the hottest summers on record. Even the sheep were suffering heat fatigue. We were dripping wet, stripping off our clothes. I got this mad feeling. I started running and screaming. He chased me. He caught me and pulled me down and we had a very unexpected fuck on the coarse grass right there and then. Just like in Lady Chatterley's Lover. We'd hardly touched each other up to that moment. I had grass burns on my bum for weeks afterwards, but it was worth it.' Charlie had a far-away look on her face.

'Lucy, you wanted to be a writer, if I remember rightly? Never thought of taking it up, on the quiet like?'

'That is my greatest wish. I'm waiting for something really compelling. Life is so drab and colourless right now. My mother is getting on my nerves. I need an idea shoved in my face which I can't ignore which says to me in big bold letters, this is it! Take me!'

Charlie took a big swig of her wine and started coughing.

Lucy took away the trays and rinsed the plates in the small sink.

'Can I use your loo?' On the wall of Charlie's bedroom was a large painting of a young lady in a white gown sitting unhappily in a boat. When Lucy returned to the living room she asked, 'Who was the artist of the painting in your loo? She looks so sad.'

'William Waterhouse, a latter day Pre Raphaelite. She's reason to be sad, poor girl. She's about to die from a terrible curse. No, not VD! The original's in the National Gallery. I have a great deal of time for him. He used the same model in many of his paintings. The title is, The Lady of Shalott. The story is based on a poem by Tennyson. The lady is under a spell to weave a fabulous tapestry about life. Her take on reality comes from a big mirror on the wall. She must never see life in the flesh, only by reflection. She is weaving away happily engrossed in her work when she hears a knight galloping past her window. She feels compelled to see who it is. She stops weaving and moves to the window. She sees Sir Lancelot at full tilt in all his knightly accoutrements heading for the castle which is round the bend in the river. Her mirror shatters. She realises by stopping weaving she has brought the consequences of the spell on herself. Before she dies, she climbs into her boat with her tapestry and floats out into the stream. The Knights of the Round Table see her coming and gather on the riverbank to wish her farewell.'

'Very sad indeed.'

'He painted another stunning painting using the same model. It's Ophelia on a riverbank about to throw herself into a river and commit suicide. She's in love with Hamlet and he spurns her. Turns her mind totally.'

Charlie had opened another bottle while Lucy was out of the room.

'That could be you, my girl, if you're not too careful. Another Andromeda needing rescuing. Pass me your glass. Oh Lucy.' Charlie leaned across and gave Lucy a moist hug.

'Lucy what happens if Sir Galahad in shining armour fails to materialise? Or even worse, is not what he appears to be? There are many paintings of naked maidens threatened by ghoulish dragons being saved by chivalrous knights in which the poor maiden appears more concerned with the intentions of the knight than she is of the dragon. You'll have wasted the best years of your life and must start all over again from the very beginning with a lot of catching up to make. Seven years, three times a week, four weeks in a month, twelve months in a year, that makes 1008 bonks you've missed so far.'

'I'll have to make up for lost time somehow.'

'You certainly will, young lady. Is the little box with the red velvet lining going to India?'

'Of course it is!' Lucy had a smug look on her face. Charlie laughed.

'There's hope for you yet! And now, let me show you what I have in my little box, what my sponsors have given me.' Charlie opened the big white cardboard box which had sat sphinx-like on the table. She drew out something that looked like a space rocket. It was a Hitachi vibrator.

'This Lucy, is the real thing. It's cordless, as you see. Rechargeable from the mains. Put it against your cheek. Feel how powerful it is!' Charlie switched it on.

'What on earth do you do with it?'

'Lucy! There's nothing you can't do with this baby. It can really shiver your timbers, believe me!'

Lucy still had a puzzled look on her face. Charlie was incapable of supplying any more information about the Hitachi's capabilities at that late hour. There was a long silence.

'Oh my God. Look at the time! Why don't you sleep here tonight? I'll make up the bed in the spare room for you. Let's shift the ironing off the bed and open the window. My Jamaican cleaning lady, Clementine, is off having another baby, number five. She's a Rastafarian, so the place is a bit of a mess.'

'I'd better call mother and set her mind at rest that I haven't been raped or anything like that. She always worries about me.'

'Of course, you do that!'

'Charlie, thanks for a splendid evening. Just what I needed.'

'We should have these evenings more often. Sleep well. There's a spare toothbrush in the cabinet in the bathroom. Come on Oscar, time for a pee, you fat boy. Now, none of that. No scratching. Stop!'

LUCYS' STRATAGEM

My name is Lucy. I am sixteen years old, and a virgin. At this time, all my friends are losing their virginity. From what they tell me, in most cases they were not even aware of it happening. They were usually too drunk to notice. To me, that is too appalling. How can someone not be aware of that moment? That very special moment which only happens to a woman once in her life. This is the story of how I planned to lose MY virginity. It would definitely NOT be an accident, or a chance happening. It would be very, very carefully planned: in every minute detail!

My aim is to wait a few years then write how I felt having lost my virginity, so that I can compare the two states. What I am writing now will go into a box, and I will lock it away until the right time to re-address the issue arises. Into the box will also go the knickers I wore for the big event.

The box was a piggybank I had bought at a gift shop. I covered the outside with white silk and the inside with crimson velvet material. It had a small padlock. I wear the key around my neck as a constant reminder.

I had given a lot of thought to the whole issue of virginity, past and present. I had read loads of books about it.

How critical it was to the Catholic church that Mary who had been chosen to bear Jesus Christ who would redeem the sins of the whole world was a virgin. To even believe that such a condition was possible, could be possible, took a considerable amount of engineering.

At the time of King Arthur, virginity was sacred. Between a young queen and her spouse in the act of defloration had to be witnessed by a court official to ensure the marriage was properly consummated. Think of Henry the Eighth and what his poor brides went through. This was so that any progeny could be absolutely verified as the issue of the king.

In Muslim countries the brothers of a young bride wait outside the door of the nuptial chamber and if the husband is not able to produce a blood-stained sheet after the act, they are allowed to cut their sister's throat. The shame of having a sister who was not absolutely pure was too much to bear.

Why had all this changed?

I wondered if I would bleed. It would be nice if I did. This was why it was important to wear white knickers so that if I did bleed it would show. Would it hurt? If I was to bleed, then most likely it would also hurt. A bit. But the passion of the moment would be so overwhelming that I would not notice. I hoped so.

Did I have any strong feelings about being a virgin? Afterwards would I feel any different?

I would often lie awake at night and try and picture how I conceived myself as a woman. Afterwards I tried to extract from this image any feelings I had that related to my virgin state. It was quite difficult at first. However, the more I thought about it, I began to perceive myself in an idealistic state. That is what the little box containing my knickers was for. After so many years had passed, I would open the box and inspect the contents. With the passage of time, I would be in a position to compare my feelings.

I thought a great deal about the right male for the act. The act of deflowerment. My knight in shining armour. I did not want to know his name. There would be no emotional attachment on either side. He would be purely an instrument. Once it was over, I wanted nothing more to do with him. I visited several school sporting events and studied the males. The first was a rugby match. I found the boys too heavy and most of them were also very hairy – hairy chests, hairy arms and legs. Hair revolted me. It also suggested a bad smell too. Tennis players were pretty good. But finally, I settled for the smooth skins, hard muscles, and flat stomachs of the swimmers. They appeared almost hairless. Aerodynamic. The hair on their heads was also cut short. The added advantage of the swimmers was that I was able to gauge the size of their sexual apparatus when they emerged from the water, their costumes clinging to their bodies. Swimmers had the sort of bodies preferred by the ancient Greeks for their Gods and heroes. The ones depicted in their statues. I had admired several during art history.

There was one swimmer I preferred to all the others. He had black hair, was a little shorter and less muscular and seemed a bit shy. He had nice, rounded shoulders with good biceps, a chest that was broad and deep but not too developed and a flat stomach. His bottom was firm and nicely rounded. From behind he had strong shoulder blades with a deep cleft between his hips. He had no hair on his chest and very little on his arms. He had long eyelashes. I decided he was the one.

What about my own body hair? Having once watched a pornographic movie I was surprised that the models, if that is what they were called, shaved their pubic hair. I found that slightly ludicrous and un-natural. No, I would trim my pubic hair slightly but leave most of it as it should be. My armpits of course would be smooth and also my legs. Not that I had much. Ladies in Pre-Raphaelite paintings had long flowing hair that reached their waists. The hair was often golden coloured. My hair was blonde and reached just below my ears. There was nothing much I could do about changing it in the short term, so I put it out of my mind.

One major problem was that the male I chose would most probably have a steady girlfriend who would object to him doing it with me. How was I going to convince him to take part in my deflowering without appearing like a trollop out for a quick bonk? My estimation of most males was that they would never turn down an offer of sex no matter what the circumstances. I was, after all, considered quite pretty and my body had all the right curves, in all the right places. At any rate, that is what my mother told me. Another thought was that if the male was totally inept, would he be able to do the deed efficiently without a lot of fuss? Better if he was in a permanent relationship and knew his way around a woman's body. I wanted the act of deflowering to be swift and clinical, without any fumbling. Once it was over there would be no sentimental mooning.

How would I entice him into taking part in the ceremony? Eventually, after much thought, I decided honesty was the best approach. I wrote him a letter stating exactly what I wanted giving him a list of terms so that he would have no false perceptions about what I had in mind. I sent a deodorant with the letter.

Next, where would it take place and when? I wanted it to be outside in daylight. That was a difficult challenge. I did not want to be watched by some sick voyeur or raped by a passerby who happened to come past at the wrong time. I spent several weekends walking in the vicinity of home trying to select just the right place. I looked at abandoned orchards but always there were one or two people about. The place had to be secluded without being home to hobos. Eventually I found a house that belonged to friends of ours who spent half the year in Malta. There was a metal gate into the garden which I found a key for. At the bottom of the garden was a small apple orchard. The orchard flattened out slightly before descending steeply to an abrupt halt at a high red-brick wall which followed the riverbank. Between the wall and the river there was a narrow pathway.

Amongst the apple trees there was a small clearing, just enough for a blanket with overgrown bushes forming a solid wall around. I decided on a blanket because though the ground was covered with grass and the soil was slightly damp.

What would I wear? I considered trousers un-ladylike and vulgar. It would have to be a dress – easy to undo with a separate bodice that unbuttoned down the front. The knickers simple white cotton. Nothing frilly or vulgar. Definitely not black or red. Certainly not red. My bra would also be white. Simple, with a few bows here and there and not too much padding. Elegant, feminine, and tasteful.

I WAS THE LADY OF SHALOTT

The time of the month was also important. I certainly did not want to be having my period. Nor did I want it to be at a time when I was most likely to get pregnant. I would of course take precautions. A condom was not right for the occasion. They smelt awful. I had handled one. Putting the thing on at the right moment would also interrupt the flow. I decided on a morning after pill. Getting one was not easy. I had a friend who had been given several by mistake. I read the instructions carefully, to be absolutely sure of avoiding pregnancy.

I wanted my knight to be dressed appropriately and to be clean and smelling nice. I went to a large department store and spent a long time savouring a vast selection of male deodorants until I chose one I liked. I bought the smallest available as I did not have much money. Did I want it gift-wrapped? I said no, feeling a little embarrassed when the salesperson looked at me and smiled.

I arranged to meet him at three in the afternoon on the twelfth day of July. It was school holidays. I knew he was not going away as his class had exams coming up and he would be sure to be swotting for them. He was to meet me at the nearest bus stop to our house. Would he arrive on time? I waited for the bus which I had calculated he would take. Would he be on the bus? He was. I had briefed him what to wear. He looked great, just as I had visualised it. He smiled as he got off the bus. I smiled back. I led the way. He followed.

In case of nerves, I had bought a bottle of red wine. I had placed this and two crystal glasses in a basket next to the blanket at the spot. I had taken out the cork in advance. I had checked everything long before he was due to arrive. Shadows from the apple trees dappled the blanket so that it was shady and cool. From all directions the spot was invisible. The weather was fine and warm. Not a cloud in the sky. Perfect conditions for the event.

He was on time. I could hear his bus arrive. I could hear his footsteps on the hard pavement. He was wearing leather shoes. Not trainers. I went out to the gate. There he was!

I immediately took his hand to dispel any nervousness. He took it without any hesitation or reluctance. I was in control. Everything was working out just right. I unlocked the gate and relocked it after we were through.

I took his hand again. We didn't speak. At the blanket I knelt down. He sat down beside me. I brought the basket over which had the wine and glasses and removed the bottle. I needed to look into his eyes. By doing this I would see whether his feelings for me were genuine or not.

He grabbed my neck and started kissing me. It was then that I smelt the alcohol on his breath. I pulled away and stood up...

I was the Lady of Shalott

Lucy got home late the following morning. As she let herself in through the front door her mother called out.

'Is that you Lucy?'

'Hullo mother. It's only me. How was your evening?'

Lucy walked down the corridor to her mother's end of the house. Her mother was sitting in her favourite chair facing the television with a lampstand beside her. The large windows that looked out onto the rose garden were behind her with their thick blue curtains drawn back. On the walls were prints of hunting scenes. On a table beside her which held all the farming magazines and old newspapers were a series of family photographs.

'I was so worried.'

'Oh Mother. You worry too much. I did call to say I was staying over with Charlie.'

'I know, but I do worry when you are out with Charlie. She's such a wild creature. I don't know what you see in her.'

'Oh mother. You do exaggerate! Charlie is a bit unconventional, but she manages, and I enjoy being with her.'

'What you're saying is that you find my company boring. I know. I'm old and dull. Don't know how your father managed for so long. I do miss him.'

'We all do. Now don't start feeling sorry for yourself. Think about the wedding. How exciting India will be. A complete change. So exciting!'

'Oh God! Don't mention the wedding. Too much to think about. The farm. What to wear.'

'Mother! Owen is quite capable of looking after the farm while we are away. You know he is. I can sit down with you and make a list of the things you need to take. It won't take long.'

Lucy's mother picked up a small photograph with an ornate frame that was sitting on a table beside her chair. 'You were such a tiny wee thing. After four miscarriages I'd just about given up of ever having my own baby. That was when we adopted Michael. And then you appeared. Such a bright little thing you were and so beautiful from the very beginning. Lucy's mother held the photograph in her hand adoringly.

Lucy sat down on the sofa and waited her moment. 'Shall I make some tea mother?'

'That would be nice.'

Lucy went through the familiar routine. Brought down the biscuit tin and put five assorted biscuits onto a small plate. When the kettle boiled, she poured hot water into the teapot and let it rest for a few minutes before placing three teaspoons of tea into the pot and putting the knitted tea-cosy on top. Her mother would not drink tea out of a mug, so Lucy placed her favourite cup on a saucer along with the small jug of fresh milk on the tray with the sugar lumps. The milk jug had a beaded net made by her mother to keep out the flies.

'You pour, mother.'

'I know you've got something to tell me about this wedding. I just know from the tone of your voice there's something more I have to deal with on top of everything else on my plate. It's really too much. I don't know how I'm going to cope. Thank goodness you'll be with me for the journey over.'

'Mother, take it easy. Don't get excited now. I've been thinking about just that. I spoke to Aunty Mary who thinks it would be better if you spend the night before the flight with them. They're seasoned travellers and know the easiest and quickest way to get to the airport from here. She and Uncle Peter and Veronica are hiring a cab which will take you all to London and the airport. Much easier than catching a train.'

'And how are you getting to the airport?'

'Mother, Charlie and I are leaving here a few days earlier. She's won a prize for two at a classy hotel in Thailand which is on the way to India. We'll come to the wedding after that. Its only four nights. Thailand is just a couple of hours from India. Like taking the train from Exeter to London.

'That Charlie. I knew she would upset everything with her harum-scarum ways.'

'Don't be unkind. We'll catch up with you and the rest of the family in good time. Never fear. All will be well.'

They hugged. Her mother started crying.

On the Monday just before eight, there was a loud thumping sound against the door of the office. Lucy had arranged to have a talk with Owen their farm manager. Jess, Owen's elderly Border Collie was at the door in good time for the meeting.

Lucy opened the door. Away in the distance the baaing of sheep could be heard. Sparrows chattered from the guttering. Rooks circled in an untidy spiral above the buildings.

'Hullo Jess. How're you this morning?' Jess wagged her bushy tail when she heard Lucy's voice and grinned, showing a grey muzzle and a mouth studded with well-worn teeth and a pink tongue. She had an arthritic hip which caused her to drag her right foot slightly.

Owen appeared round the corner of the house wearing his usual farm apparel, blue jeans, Wellington boots, long-sleeved blue shirt, and quilted Barbour jacket with tweed cap. He carried a stout wooden crook.

'Morning Owen. It's a lovely day. Why don't we go for a walk. We can talk at the same time?'

'Splendid idea. I can show you the new lambs about ready to go t'market.'

They went out of the gate into the lane which took them over an old brick bridge that spanned the stream. Below the bridge the river broadened out into a pond where there was an assortment of duck and geese. As they came over the bridge a flock of wild mallard took off, wheeled and zoomed off over the willows that grew beside the pond at the far end. They made a high circuit above their heads, the drake quacking loudly. Following a hedgerow up a gentle slope they reached a metal gate into a large meadow where the sheep were. The meadow was flat and stretched away to a small coppice of trees on the skyline where a flock of rooks wheeled. Several fat wood pigeons rose up from the meadow with a clatter of wings and flew off towards the trees. In the distance a pheasant called reminding Lucy of rusty clockwork. Alongside each sheep were two stout lambs nearly as tall as their mother. When the ewes spotted Jess, they called their lambs to them. The nearest lambs started baaing and disappeared under the broad belly of their dame. Jess sidled up to one group and began to herd them, her head held low, eyes glued on the ewe. Owen whistled.

'Get back, Jess.'

Jess dropped to the ground looking at Owen out of the corner of her eye for further instructions.

'Anything you need before I leave?'

'No, I've everything. Booked abattoir to collect lambs Friday.'

'That's good.'

'Farm's running very smoothly now, thanks to that Dad of yours. You should be very proud of him. He worked night and day for many long years to create this farm with the sweat of his body. Never had a day off in thirty years, with occasional visits to agricultural fairs and so on. What you can see here is the fruits of all that work. It probably killed him in the end. He was always very proud of you.'

Lucy had an image of her father striding across the paddock, the rain streaming down his face carrying a bale of hay balanced on his shoulders to take to a ewe that had dislocated her hip and was being fed in a temporary shelter her father had constructed against the drystone wall of the paddock until the vet could come and see to it. The stream had flooded its banks and all roads into the farm were blocked.

'You had a lot to do with that too, Owen, don't count yourself out.'

'We were a good team. I enjoyed working with your Dad. How's your Mum?'

'Not so good at the moment. The wedding in Kolkata is proving too much for her.'

'She thought the world of your Dad. When he died so sudden, it knocked her back something terrible.'

'She still hasn't come to terms with it. He did everything for her. She relied on him for everything. She couldn't even sign a cheque or draw money from the bank.'

'Well now Lucy, you go and enjoy yourself. I can handle everything nicely while you are away. You need have no worries on't. Do you want me to do anything? I can drive your mother to station if you want?'

'Owen, that's very kind of you. Don't worry about that. My uncle has arranged all that.'

'You take it easy too. And have some fun for a change. Get out and see something of the world, Lucy.'

Lucy reached out and took Owen's hard dry hand in hers and squeezed it. 'Don't worry about me.'

As Lucy walked back to the house Jess trotted after her. Lucy turned to see where Owen was and pointed Jess in his direction.

'There he is. Off you go!'

Owen whistled. Jess pricked up her long ears, turned, and was off in a few neat bounds, tail low, sleek body hugging the ground like a surface-to-surface missile.

Later that morning Lucy took her horse Blaze out for a ride. He was out in the meadow with her mother's horse, Amber. He was big, had been hunted and when Lucy saw him for the first time, she felt he was far too big and strong for her. Opinion amongst the local horse fraternity agreed with this, but Lucy liked him from the start, and wouldn't be dissuaded. She felt confident she could gain his respect and affection, and they had hit it off from the very beginning. He was called Blaze because down his forehead he had a vivid white streak like a lightning bolt. As Lucy approached the paddock, he spotted her and trotted over. Lucy always got a thrill when he responded to her in this way. She ran her hand down his broad flat forehead feeling the hard bone beneath the skin. She ran the back of her hand down his nose between his nostrils feeling the velvet soft skin and allowed him to nuzzle her throat. She caught a strong whiff of him. An aroma that combined the scent of meadow flowers, oats, wet earth, with his own sweat that was not like human sweat but was much more organic and animal. She loved it.

'Blaze dear boy. You are too gorgeous for words.' She made incoherent mumbling sounds, her way of indicating that she enjoyed his caresses as much as she enjoyed caressing him. He cheekily pushed his nose down into her crotch in search of a horse cube and she felt his hot breath against her thigh through the fabric of her jodhpurs and his wiry whiskers tickled.

'Blaze, naughty boy.' To avoid his questing mouth, she swivelled her hips and shoved her hand into her pocket and found a cube, and held it out for him. He stuck out his long, wet tongue and searched in the hollows of her hand, and with her help got the cube into his mouth which he crunched with his powerful molars.

'Come on, now.'

She patted his powerful neck, took hold of his halter, and lead him out of the paddock to the barn where she kept her tack. His iron-shod hooves click-clacked against the hard surface of the lane. Saddled up, she trotted out of the yard down the hill to a stretch of low-lying meadow which ran alongside a weed-choked stream popular with moorhen and coot.

As a heron rose from the reeds, Blaze put his ears forward and reared. He summed up the scene in a trice, and before Lucy could stop him, he broke into a canter. Lucy sensed his urgency and pulled back on the reins to slow him. The heron flew languidly along the stream until it alighted in a dead tree.

Close to the stream, the slope levelled, and as they reached a narrow muddy track that ran parallel to the stream, Lucy relaxed the reigns and allowed Blaze to surge forward in a full gallop. Lucy gripped tightly with her thighs and calves and leant forward so that her chin was just touching Blaze's neck, the pommel of the saddle thudding against her groin.

As Blaze settled into his stride Lucy surrendered herself and allowed her brain to disconnect. She was aware of the rhythm of the thudding hooves and the wind over her ears and the feel of the powerful animal moving between her thighs. She visualised the beach with the waves just breaking on the shore. The sun emerging through the cloud bank and catching the curl of the waves as it cascaded onto the beach. Out of the sea-mist emerged a dark creature that grew larger rapidly. It was a black horse with mane trailing in the wind approaching with enormous strides, its eyes glowed like red-hot coals, like the horse in Henry Fuseli's Nightmare painting. Lucy was not sure whether to be excited or afraid. What she did know was that she wanted to be associated with it. She reached out, but it thundered past and disappeared into the mist.

After she had changed out of her jodhpurs and had a shower, she sat and had a cup of tea. It was then that she felt fluid dribbling down one leg. She ran a finger up her calf and studied it. Then she knew!

Lucy spent the rest of the day with her mother until she could barely stand another moment. Lucy got so fed up that she made up her mind to accept Charlie's plan to stop off in Bangkok en-route for the wedding, no matter what. She phoned Charlie to tell her.

'Charlie, Bangkok is on?' All she heard was hysterical laughter. She still had to find a way of making peace with her mother. A daunting challenge!

That evening Lucy began packing and realised that apart from her wedding apparel she had nothing suitable to take to Thailand. In a panic she drove to the nearest Marks and Spencers where she was able to buy enough hot weather clothing for Thailand and India.

She packed as she had seen her mother pack. One set of clothes for each day of the holiday in layers. For their first day in Bangkok Lucy imagined heat and humidity. First a pair of white cotton knickers which she always wore with a plain white bra to go with which had a tiny yellow bow between the cups like a cowslip. One of her new tops from M&S. A pair of knee-high slacks which matched the top. A pair of leather sandals. In case a swim offered, she put in her one-piece swimsuit which was pretty old but fitted her well. For hot nights two light-weight nighties. Her Teddy Bear eyed her from its position on her pillows. A gift from her mother when she was five years old when she and her brother were left for a week with their uncle and aunt when their parents went on a special holiday to Spain. Why not? He took up no room and was very light. She squeezed him in between two pairs of shoes. Lucy had a thing about handbags. She decided to take a small black backpack in which she could keep her wallet and travel documents safely.

Charlie was in London meeting with the editor of her magazine so would go to the airport separately. They were to meet in the departure lounge. Charlie called Lucy to say she was going to be late. The underground station she had chosen which linked to the Piccadilly Line and Heathrow Airport was closed due to a bomb scare.

Lucy's two suitcases fitted easily into the luggage bins at one end of the carriage. The train was not very full being mid-afternoon. She found two empty seats facing the engine and sat in the one nearest the window. As the familiar countryside flashed past the window Lucy felt comforted. This was the world she had grown up in, and which she was familiar with. She found the jog-jog rhythm of the train soothing, and very soon she dozed off in the knowledge that it was impossible to sleep through.

She was woken by the refreshments trolley. She decided to buy some sandwiches and a fruit juice. The train slowed as it neared Waterloo. At Waterloo, Lucy headed for the Underground. Not knowing how to buy a ticket from the machines, she queued at the ticket office. An elderly Asian gentleman helped her buy her ticket. This took a little time as there were several young people with backpacks new to travel in England. From there it was down a long escalator with her eyes peeled for a Northern Line train to Charing Cross where she had to change again for a Piccadilly line train to Heathrow Airport and Terminal Two. Charlie had warned her about getting out at the right terminal as there were at least four of them. Lucy was very grateful that both her suitcases had wheels. As the doors opened at the Terminal Two platform, Lucy pulled down her two bags and stepped briskly out of the train and headed for the escalator signposted for Departures. As the escalator emerged into the enormous Departures Hall, Lucy's phone rang. It was Charlie to say she was still trying to get a taxi. She was going to be late. A wave of panic went through Lucy. How was she ever going to make it through all on her own without Charlie? She didn't even know which airline they were travelling on. She found a spot behind a row of chairs and searched for her ticket. She found her flight number. British Airways. Looking around she spotted the British Airways departure desk. There was a long queue which she joined.

Lucy had never flown in an airplane in her life. What most people take for granted was to her novel. First the security checks with shoes off and all hand luggage posted through an X-ray machine. Nobody told her about liquids in her carry-on luggage and a bottle of moisturiser was found in her bag which had to be removed, along with a pair of nail-scissors. She was most upset about losing the scissors.

THEODORA PERFECT

The plane circled over the city as it made its final approach. Lucy could see through her window the main river and the canals set out in a herring-bone pattern with the sun glinting on the water, and numerous modern skyscrapers jostling for position. When the plane had come to a standstill and the doors were opened, there was a blast of hot pungent air which ruffled her hair and sucked the breath from her lungs. The dazzling bright sunlight made her squint. The passengers climbed aboard a bus and Lucy could feel her clothes clinging to her body. The sky was overcast which absorbed some of the sun's heat, but the intensity of light was hard to get used to. Lucy wished she had bought a pair of sunglasses. Some of the passengers had fans. As it was Lucy's first time on a plane, arriving at the airport building was confusing. She picked out one or two passengers from her plane and followed them to the immigration desks where she selected the non-Thai passport holders' queue. A smart young immigration official wearing a spotless white shirt and epaulettes stamped her passport and wished her a happy stay. After that she followed other passengers from her flight who knew the ropes, and were marching purposefully towards the baggage reclaim area. They went down some escalators into a large hall. She caught sight of her flight number on a board and found herself waiting beside a conveyor belt. She spotted her suitcase, which had been her mother's, doing the rounds. It had a length of pink wool tied to the handle. She pulled it off as it went past and looked for a luggage trolley. After that it was customs and the green route, and she was through.

Away from the air conditioning of the airport building, Lucy was sweating already and needed to change into something cooler. Coming out from Customs she was faced by an array of people holding placards which bore the names of arriving guests. She scanned them and spotted a young lady holding one with Lucy and Charlie, welcome to Bangkok on it. Lucy waved and made her way towards the lady who had a big smile on her face, wearing sunglasses perched on the top of her head. Lucy shook hands with the lady. She wanted to know where Charlie was as she had a small gift for her. Lucy explained that Charlie would be arriving the next day. The lady spoke on her phone for a few seconds. A small bus appeared. They set off. The air-conditioning was a relief.

The traffic was frenetic. After orderly London and the quiet lanes of Somerset with its manicured hedgerows where you might meet a tractor or a delivery van occasionally, this was pure bedlam. Three-wheeler motor scooters called Tuk Tuks zoomed in and out of the traffic like skateboarders. Tall modern skyscrapers that can be found in any modern city soared into the dazzling sky wherever Lucy looked.

In no time at all the bus drew over beside a canal. Several wooden brightly painted long-tailed boats with steeply raised prows were tied up to the dock. The driver leapt out briskly, gave a loud shout, whereupon one of the boat pilots spotted them and waved. He hurried across and picked up Lucy's luggage and stored it aboard. Lucy was shown where to sit to avoid the spray from the bows. The water smelt like a cattle barn on a hot summer's day. The boat had a red and blue canvas awning. Once they were under way the breeze was a pleasant relief from the oppressive heat. It was a short fast ride to the hotel which overlooked the canal. Going by boat was much easier than going by taxi. There were regular traffic jams. It gave Lucy a marvellous opportunity of getting the geography of the city into her mind. The canal connected with the main river. Lucy was led to reception and given a warm greeting by the staff. The hotel was not one of the most modern ones and not grand either. It was friendly and well positioned to reach the various places of interest. In their room was a big bowl of flowers. On a table by the wall was a bowl of tropical fruit. On each bed was an ornate design made from poinsettia flowers welcoming them to the hotel.

That evening Lucy ate a simple meal at the hotel and studied what Charlie had printed out for them to do the following day. She had down for the Tuesday a visit to the Wat Pho reclining Buddha temple.

THEODORA PERFECT

She left the doors onto the balcony open so that she could hear the city through the window. Above the sound of the traffic below she could hear crows calling to one another. She dropped the mosquito net. The air-conditioning was on full blast, but it was barely noticeable.

The following morning Lucy left the hotel early, before rush-hour and climbed aboard a boat which took her to a wharf adjacent to the monastery. She bought a ticket for the monastery which included a massage. It indicated a time. There was lots of time for a walk around the monastery first.

As it was still early, there were very few tourists in the temple. She followed a small group and arrived at the reclining Buddha itself. It was enormous. About as long as five London double-decker buses. It was very difficult to get it all into the frame of her camera. She could only do this by standing well back against the wall. In the distance she could hear male voices chanting from the temple itself. She walked towards the sound and reached the doorway to the temple.

Outside two elaborately carved wooden doors were rows and rows of shoes of various sizes and styles. She knelt and took off her sandals and tucked them between a pair of pink trainers so that she could easily find them again. She found herself right at the back of the temple itself. A religious ceremony was in progress. Lucy walked cautiously forward and squatted on a thick red carpet behind a group of tourists on the right side of the temple. She was struck at first sight by a golden Buddha that sat on a high platform at the back of the hall. An enormous cone-shaped lamp cast a very bright beam of golden light onto the Buddha. Supporting the roof running along each side of the temple area were two rows of very tall rectangular columns. These were all ornamented with intricate scenes. Kneeling on a raised platform that ran all the way to the front of the building and covered in a thick red carpet, were rows and rows of kneeling monks in their crimson and gold gowns. Their right arms were bare.

Some held small books in their hands from which they read the text of the chants. All had shaved heads. Some were very young, about fourteen and fifteen. The air was filled with incense which rose up in a thick blue cloud so that the ceiling was obscured. Up near the altar, one or two people were beating gongs and cymbals. A monk was leading a chant in a deep bass voice that reverberated round the whole building.

The scene filled her with wonder and amazement. There was an atmosphere of profound spirituality. She had never ever felt so moved when visiting cathedrals and holy places in England. This was very different. The stillness, the smell of centuries of incense. There was something deep and sincere in the attitude of the monks to their religion. They really looked as if they believed wholeheartedly in what they were doing. There was nothing half-hearted about it. Every atom of their being was focused on what they were doing.

She studied the faces of the monks kneeling to her left. One of them was older than his colleagues. She didn't know exactly why he attracted her. Maybe it was the way he carried himself. He had a patrician appearance and expressed pride in himself. He was in his forties and taller than the other monks. His skin was paler. His head was shaved which revealed his clear-cut features. He had an athletic build. Like a basketball player. Very like a swimmer. His right arm that was not covered by his robe was muscular, like an athlete's. He reminded her of early photos of the Dalai Lama. In short, Lucy was totally enthralled by him. She couldn't help gazing at him. He was absorbed in what he was doing. However, at some point he turned his head very slightly and caught sight of her. It was almost as if he felt the energy of her interest in him. Their eyes made contact for the briefest of moments. She was the one who broke the contact. His power was too much for her. She had to look away. She was bowled over. She looked at her watch and realised that her massage was minutes away. She stood up and walked to the exit. At the door she stopped, turned, and took a photo.

Lucy left the temple. There was quite a long queue for the

massage. She showed her ticket and was shown to a row of benches. She sat down next to an elderly man with a brightly coloured T-shirt with Mickey Mouse printed on the front. While she waited, several monks walked by. She studied them to see if she could catch sight of him again, but she was disappointed. Her turn came and she stood up and walked towards a vacant bed. She was given a robe of strong cotton to wear over her clothes. While she was having her massage and thinking of him, she saw him standing at the railings. This was a shock. He was not aware that she could see him. She was lying on her stomach with her arms facing forwards on either side of her ears. Her hair screened her view.

After her massage, she felt quite spaced out and very hungry. As she stood up to take off her robe, she looked around to see if she could see him, but he was nowhere to be seen. She decided to head for the Lumpini Gardens and eat at an outdoor restaurant and watch the ducks swimming on the lake. She loved the pink waterlilies. On the succulent emerald-green grass a group of middle-aged people was having a Tai Chi lesson. There were large white carp with pink and golden markings gliding about in the lake. Green and gold swallow-tail butterflies hovered momentarily above frangipani blossoms.

When she got back to her hotel Charlie was unpacking her suitcase. She looked up in surprise as Lucy closed the door. 'Lucy!'

'Charlie. You made it.'

Charlie rushed up to Lucy and hugged her. 'I'm so sorry. I've been worried sick about you. Tell me what you've been up to. How've you got on? Isn't it a great place? You're alive, and well. That's the great thing. Nothing terrible has happened, has it?'

While she was speaking Charlie looked anxiously at Lucy. 'Has it?'

Lucy studied her fingernails, tugged at the lobe of one ear, closed her eyes and shook her head, 'No, of course not. Why should it?' She let out a very deep sigh. 'It's hard to explain. It's nothing I could ever have imagined. There's just too much to take in all at once.'

'Yes, yes I know. It hasn't overwhelmed you in any way, though? That's what I was worried about. You being out of your comfort zone and panicking. Why it was so important I was here with you at the very beginning. To cushion you, if you fell.'

'It is overwhelming. Yes, of course it is. There's just so much going on, all at once, and so very different. The frenzied bustle of traffic and the noise, not to mention the heat and the humidity. The sunlight. I feel I need to change my clothes every half hour. So different to what we're used to in dreary old England.'

'Yes. Oh Lucy!' Charlie hugged Lucy again. Nothing more was said.

'You shower first Charlie.'

'Are you sure? I won't take long.' Charlie burrowed into her suitcase which lay on one of the beds and dragged out a battered toilet bag and a sarong. Undressing quickly, she draped the sarong around her shoulders and disappeared into the shower, clutching her toilet bag as if it contained stolen treasure. Very soon through the sound of gushing water could be heard Charlie singing. Not long after, the door opened, followed by clouds of steam. Charlie emerged wearing her sarong, leaving wet footprints on the tiled floor, and smelling strongly of unguents and lotions courtesy of the hotel.

Lucy showered quickly, and afterwards arranged her own toiletries tidily on one shelf of the wall cabinet. When she came out, Charlie had changed into her tropical outfit: floral shorts, a saffron coloured blouse with short sleeves, and leather sandals. She had brushed her hair so that it cascaded over her shoulders.

They went out for a meal. As they headed for their restaurant, Lucy was grateful that with all the noise of the traffic it was very difficult to talk. She relaxed a bit and began to take in her surroundings.

Lucy was relieved that Charlie found a very traditional restaurant with dim lighting. They had the place all to themselves. On their table was a crimson orchid in a cut glass vase. Against the wall was an aquarium with several goldfish with extended bellies and trailing fins like Thai dancers. Traditional music was playing in the background.

The air-conditioning was up high.

Charlie wanted to have a soapy massage. They took a pink taxi to Ratchadaphisek Road, the narrow street which was in the heart of the massage district. On the way Charlie described what a soapy massage was all about.

The girls sit in a circle in what was known as the fishbowl. They have their names on their dresses. Clients can study them through a glass window and pick the one they desire.

Charlie picked out a girl she fancied. Having a massage was the very last thing on earth Lucy wanted. She would sit and wait for Charlie. While she was doing this, she flicked through her photos. She found the ones taken in the monastery. She anxiously scanned the images.

At that moment, who came in through the door but the very person she was thinking about? Lucy recognised him immediately. He went up to the receptionist and spoke to her. She seemed to know him. She picked up a phone and dialled a number. While this was going on he turned towards Lucy. He looked straight at her for a few seconds. Lucy blushed and looked at her feet. She had an overpowering feeling she was going to pass out. He was wearing western clothes. From one of the cubicles a young Thai girl appeared and went up to him. They spoke in friendly terms. She put her hand on his elbow and drew him away from reception. They brushed past Lucy. In the process he dropped something. Lucy bent down to see what had been dropped. She found it, picked it up and popped it into her pocket. They returned soon after, and he said good-bye to the girl and left. The girl watched him go, then turned. Her eyes were glowing intensely. She saw Lucy and smiled. Without hesitating she came up and said in a cheerful tone, 'Shall we go?'

Lucy was taken by surprise. Suddenly all her reservations about having a massage vanished. She got up hastily and followed the girl, who halted outside the door of one of the rooms. She ushered Lucy in and locked the door. The floor was tiled. The tiles reached half-way up the walls. Along one wall was an enormous bath. Beside it a shower, beyond that a toilet. Facing the bath along the opposite wall was a double blow-up Lilo. She introduced herself.

'Hi, my name Chimlin.'

She ran water into the bath. While the water was running, and the steam was rising she led Lucy to a corner of the room where she suggested Lucy took off her clothes. Lucy hung her clothes on pegs on the wall. Chimlin beckoned to Lucy. Lucy walked totally naked and embarrassed towards the bath. Meanwhile, Chimlin did a quick scan of the salient points of Lucy's anatomy. Lucy climbed in gingerly. The water was just right. Lucy lay back. Chimlin removed her clothes and joined Lucy in the bath.

Chimlin's skin was golden brown, her body lean and strong with not an ounce of fat. It was not a beautiful body in the western sense. It was a working body. She was shorter than Lucy. Her long raven-black hair was tied in a ponytail above her ears with a silver hair clip. She had small jade earrings. Chimlin, being careful not to tread on Lucy, squatted beside her right hip. She filled a big pink sponge with soap from a dispenser and began soaping Lucy. She started at her throat, rubbing gently in circular movements down to her right breast. She rubbed it gently. She paid special attention to the nipple which was standing proud. She moved to the other breast. Lucy closed her eyes and tried to concentrate on the sensations. The stress which had built up during her flight to Bangkok, missing Charlie, and dealing with her mother, began to disperse. Chimlin was now leaning over Lucy. Their bodies nearly touching. Lucy touched Chimlin's firm breast with her fingertips. Her nipples reminded her of ripe raisins. The areolas like penny coins. Lucy raised herself so that she could nuzzle the nipple with her nose. Chimlin did not respond. Lucy sighed. Chimlin giggled and tapped her on the nose with the sponge. Soap went up Lucy's nose and she sneezed. Chimlin burst out laughing. Lucy sneezed several more times and couldn't stop laughing. Chimlin found a tissue and gave it to Lucy to blow her nose. When she had finished, she took it and put it in a bin beside the bath.

Chimlin squirted more soap onto the sponge and continued. She put one hand on Lucy's sternum and pushed her back gently, moving the sponge across her stomach, over her belly button, across both hips in a broad circular motion. At the apex of her belly, she changed direction and moved up and back. She swished the sponge in the water and wiped the bubbles away. Lucy closed her eyes. The sponge moved down between her thighs and Lucy spread them to make it easier for her. Lucy felt the blood move to her extremities. She became aware of her nostrils and upper lip. Lucy opened her mouth to let in more air. She ran her tongue across her lower lip which felt dry. Her breathing accelerated. She opened her eyes. Their eyes met. There was a slight smile on Chimlin's lips and her eyes were sparkling.

Wanting more, Lucy lay back and raised her hips higher, careful not to let water enter her mouth. Chimlin responded by putting the sponge beside her and with one hand on the side of the bath walked her knees down the bath away from Lucy's hips. She seized Lucy's right foot and pushed her back. With Lucy's foot in her left hand, she soaped her calf. Changing the grip of Lucy's foot, she held her toes and soaped the top of her leg up to the foot, then slid the sponge between Lucy's toes one by one. After that she held Lucy's heel and rubbed the sponge up the underside of her foot very gently, moving between her toes again. From her toes the sponge moved along the top of her leg to her knee which flexed, and back to her toes. A quick rinse of the sponge and she released Lucy's left foot and took up her up right foot. She repeated the procedure.

Lucy was in a state of bliss. No thoughts, only feelings. She hardly heard the words, 'Turn over now.'

Lucy rolled over and folded her arms under her chin with her face turned to one side. She realised she could not see Chimlin's eyes. Chimlin let more water into the bath and squirted more soap onto her sponge. Her knees were once again alongside Lucy's hips.

Lucy felt the sponge on her left ear, moved down her neck, made circular movements across one shoulder then the other. The sponge moved lower across Lucy's ribs on each side, made a long sweep up her spine to the nape of her neck then down as far as the hollow at the base of her spine. It moved to the left and languidly encircled her buttock across to the other buttock, up her spine to where her shoulder blades met down again in a straight line. This time the sponge moved on down between her buttocks and further still to where her feelings were most acute. It paused there, swooshing water back and forth, creating small waves which rolled over her exposed flesh giving Lucy intense tingles of pleasure, the likes of which she had never felt before.

Chimlin changed position so that her knees were between Lucy's feet. She held Lucy's left foot and gently parted her legs. The sponge moved up the inside of Lucy's thigh to the top, the apex, where all the lines of geometry met. With more space the sponge could now work its way up the cleft in Lucy's groin and back again. When Chimlin felt Lucy could take no more, the sponge backed out to run along the top of Lucy's leg to her foot. Chimlin changed hands holding Lucy's right foot in her hand now so that the sponge could make another run up Lucy's right thigh to the very top and back again.

Lucy felt an overpowering desire to reach out and touch Chimlin. Her desire for physical contact was now so intense without it she felt she would die.

'Out now, please. We move to the mattress. Okay?'

Chimlin's words of command came to Lucy as though from another world, not from her immediate consciousness, but from somewhere far away. It took Lucy a great effort of concentration to get out of the bath.

Chimlin was out of the bath and standing beside the large, inflated mattress. She beckoned to Lucy. She had taken the bottle of soap with her, but the sponge remained beside the bath.

'Lie on your tummy first. That's it.'

Lucy lay down her arms lying loosely at her sides. Chimlin squirted liquid onto Lucy's back and rubbed it over her shoulders and down her back, between her buttocks and down her thighs. Lucy did not know what to expect. Very gently Chimlin lowered her body onto Lucy's so that she was lying on top of her. Without using her hands, she rubbed her body gently against Lucy's using her breasts as a sponge. This was the physical contact Lucy was craving, and she gave into it whole-heartedly. In addition to the pressure of her two firm breasts. Chimlin's crotch now came into play. Chimlin's crotch was smooth and devoid of any hair. She began grinding it into Lucy's buttocks, first at the top then below, pushing her hips down and in without using her hands. Lucy could hear her own breathing becoming more rapid. She held her breath between thrusts to provide more focus. Once again, she was aware of her blood moving to the surface. Her lips yearned for a soft yielding surface. The texture of the Lilo was rough and unrewarding. Chimlin forced Lucy's thighs apart so that her thrusts could be directed more at Lucy's bottom and what lay beneath. Lucy moved her body to meet Chimlin's and soon their bodies were perfectly synchronised.

All too soon Chimlin stopped and knelt at the foot of the Lilo. 'Turn over now. Other side.'

Lucy rolled over. She made contact with Chimlin's eyes. There was the same smile, in addition there was assurance, and, with it, knowledge and power.

Lucy's hands were now free to move and respond. Still Chimlin kept hers away. She started by rubbing her left breast over Lucy's face so that her lips could touch the sharp nipple. Lucy nuzzled Chimlin's breast with her nose and mouth and Chimlin giggled. Then it was the turn of the right breast. Lucy put her arms around Chimlin and pulled her down searching for her mouth and her lips. Lucy kissed her throat, and the hollow formed by her throat and her collar bone. Lucy grabbed a handful of hair and pulled Chimlin's face down to hers. Chimlin resisted and playfully tapped Lucy on the nose with her index finger disciplining her. Before Lucy could obstruct her, she had moved her breasts so that they were rubbing against Lucy's stomach. Lucy held Chimlin's head in her hands to direct its movement. As it moved slowly down Lucy's body she opened her legs. Chimlin rose in a crouch, pushed Lucy's thighs apart and brought her groin down so that it covered Lucy's. Very gently at first, Chimlin rubbed her crotch against Lucy's, first up and down then from side to side. Lucy grabbed her shoulders, then her hips. She encircled Chimlin's buttocks with her own thighs pulling her down and into her, enhancing the pressure. Chimlin started grunting. Lucy was panting. Back and forth. Back and forth. Side to side. Chimlin let out a deep groan and Lucy felt her own climax coming, like waves flooding her body from top to bottom. Lucy began to fantasise about him. She longed to place her mouth where her mouth had recently been. She leant forward and holding Chimlin's neck like an anchor she kissed her full on the lips. Her lips were soft and wet. Lucy imagined she was kissing him. She could taste him on her lips. She was close to her first orgasm. She didn't want it to stop.

Chimlin drew back, and with a hand on each knee, gently closed Lucy's thighs, like closing a book at bedtime. Lucy felt cheated. Chimlin leant forward and with her right hand behind Lucy's neck placed her lips on the centre of her forehead. Lucy wanted to regain control, but Chimlin held Lucy like that, head-to-head. When Lucy was calm, she released her head, and with her right hand she gently pushed Lucy down and looked into her eyes. Lucy felt her gaze like a laser, probing her mind, summing her up. Gauging her state. After many moments, during which Lucy's heartbeat slowed from a frantic sprint to a steady walk, when her breathing could be counted in single breaths, rather than a burst from a machine-gun, Lucy became conscious of where she was, and who she was. Chimlin's voice brought Lucy into the present, like a slap across the face.

'Enough for today. You enjoy your first massage. I think so?' Her eyebrows rose in affirmation.

Lucy nodded. Unable to look Chimlin in the eyes.

They dressed in silence. Chimlin unlocked the door, ushering Lucy out into the empty corridor like being ushered out after a dentist's appointment. In the corridor Lucy tried to seek out Chimlin's eyes, but her back was turned.

Before they reached the foyer Chimlin gave Lucy a card. Outside in the foyer Charlie was waiting. When she caught sight of Lucy her face lit up with a broad smile.

'Wow! Lucy, you look radiant, as if you've just had the most fantastic experience of your whole life.'

Lucy released her rubber hair tie allowing her hair to cascade over her face like a curtain in an attempt at nonchalance, while underneath blushing shamelessly. Having gained control, Lucy threw her head back, grabbed her hair with one hand and retied it. She started giggling. Having paid, Lucy couldn't wait to get outside into the bright sunlight amongst strangers and traffic and noise.

Charlie put her arm around Lucy's shoulders and gave her a firm sisterly hug. They walked arm in arm for a few minutes until a small lane offered some shade, relative peace, and quiet. Charlie drew Lucy aside behind a stall selling brightly coloured shawls and prayer mats.

Lucy took the opportunity to take several deep breaths. She became aware of the noise of the traffic. Above the smell of exhaust fumes was the smell of fried chicken. She had a pang of hunger.

'Now!'

'What?'

'Are you ready for this? The next thing on my bucket list is a tattoo. We're in the right part of the city for that. Khao San Road is not far from here. Let's hire a Tuk Tuk. It'll be easier with all this traffic.'

'Yes! good idea.'

Charlie spotted one coming and waved. It stopped beside them, and they climbed in. Charlie haggled for a few moments until the fare was agreed. There were only two seats, and they faced forward behind the driver. The sides were open and there was a flimsy canvas awning over their heads that flapped about once they got going. At the back of the driver's seat was an elaborate art deco design made from welded metal rods. The driver was in his early twenties and steered his motor-bike contraption in and out of the seething traffic with the same aplomb as a rugby fly-half manoeuvring around charging flankers. After a hectic ten-minute drive, they found themselves in a narrow street with neon signs flashing on either side and just enough room in the road for one car and a bicycle to pass safely. Charlie knew the tattoo artist she had in mind. Each shop provided its own brand of tattoo, and these were displayed on large glossy billboards in the windows. They reached the shop. Along one wall were padded chairs. On the opposite wall were more photos of the tattooist's work. Behind a row of curtains was a dentist's chair. The high-pitched sound of the tattoo gun could be heard. Charlie went up to a young girl sitting behind the counter and explained what she had in mind. The girl handed Charlie a grubby plastic folder which contained a selection of photos of tattoos slotted into plastic leaves in the price range Charlie could afford.

Charlie wanted to have a small tattoo that was nice and inconspicuous at the base of her spine where the Muladhara chakra lay. Kundalini, the power that transcends all others had its roots there evidently.

'I can only afford a dinky little one. You can come in and watch or glance through their catalogues.'

'I would rather sit here and wait for you. If I can't bear the sound of you squealing, I can always go for a walk.'

'Coward.'

Lucy sat on a shiny leatherette sofa the colour of dried blood. On the opposite wall were a series of framed photographs of young ladies and muscular men sporting tattoos. It was quite dark in the parlour. The young receptionist behind the counter was bent over studying her phone. Lucy crossed her legs and tried to get comfortable. That didn't work. She straightened her legs. It was then she felt moisture trickling down one leg. Then it dawned on her. Her cheeks burned. She didn't know where to look. She found her handkerchief, checked that nobody was looking, stood up, wiped her calf, and sat down again.

When it was her turn, Charlie went behind the curtain and Lucy could hear Charlie explaining what she wanted. Most tattooists use a stencil, which is stuck onto the skin and a broad outline is inked in first, using this as guidance. Very few work entirely freehand,

and those that do, are much in demand. It was not long before she heard the high-pitched sound of the tattoo gun, which sounded like a dentist's drill. She pictured Charlie's sensitive white flesh being punctured, and the agony.

When the whine of the tattoo gun stopped, there was a delay, while Charlie had a disinfectant solution rubbed over the tattoo. When she appeared, she was rather pink in the cheeks, but nonetheless happy.

'How did it go? Sounded rather painful from this side of the curtain.'

'Not too bad. After a while you begin the enjoy the pain. I suppose it's those endorphins getting to work, the ones that give runners their high.'

'Do you realise you'll never see this man's handy-work. Isn't that a bit narcissistic?'

'Who knows? Just knowing it's there is good enough for me. My special lovers will see it, after all. Won't they?'

'I suppose so. If that's how you want to be observed!'

'Lucy, it takes all sorts. You never know what might come up! Look. An underwear shop. What sort of underwear do you have? I can guess. White cotton knickers with matching bra? Let me buy you something a little more alluring as a present to match the occasion? Why not? Come on, let's have a look, even if we don't like what's on offer.' They went in.

Along both walls were photos of mannequins wearing underwear which Lucy considered fit only for strippers in a Paris night-club. She shuddered.

'Lucy, why not get a couple of black knickers with bra to match. Easy to wash and goes with anything? Lucy are you there?'

'Ok. You choose. This is not my scene.'

A young sales assistant with a large smile came up and Charlie began explaining what she had in mind. The girl disappeared into the back room and a few minutes later appeared carrying several items which she displayed on the countertop.

Charlie picked them up one by one and looked at them critically.

'These are the plainest they have. I like these. What do you think?'

'Simple, cotton, nice and cool to let your fanny breathe a bit?'

Lucy was too embarrassed to speak at first. She held up one a pair for closer scrutiny. They were very flimsy and narrower at the back.

'Those are called thongs. Very popular these days. Why not get three pairs of black and three more like a bikini with a coloured pattern. How about that?'

Lucy was not paying attention. Her thoughts were elsewhere.

The items were wrapped, and Charlie paid. 'I'm absolutely starving. I think my Muladhara chakra is already making itself known. What about grabbing something scrummy from a stall then wandering back to the hotel. We can go out later and have a proper meal in one of those restaurants near the hotel overlooking the canal.'

'Sounds perfect. Just what I was thinking.'

The following morning the sun streamed through a narrow chink in the heavy curtains. The noise of the city was muted. Charlie had already dressed by the time Lucy woke. She was tiptoeing barefoot around the bedroom putting things into her shoulder bag trying to be discrete.

Lucy turned over. It took a few moments before she realised she was not in her familiar bed back on the farm. She gave a small toss of her head as though to clear her mind. Charlie noticed and came over to stand beside her. In a loud whisper Charlie explained her timetable for the morning.

'I'm awake. You don't have to whisper.'

'Lucy, I'm going to have to leave you to your own resources this morning. I have those projects to deal with that I mentioned. Are you going to be O.K on your own? I have written down other things to do which you could check out while I'm away.'

'I'll be fine. I need to catch up on my diary.'

'Can I have a look at your phone please?'

'Its over there in my hand bag. What's wrong?'

'Nothing at all. Listen, for safety reasons I want to set it so that if you lose it somebody can find it. These modern phones are so bloody clever.'

Charlie found Lucy's phone and brought it over to the bed. 'Good, this is a nice new one and has all the latest gizmos.'

Charlie fiddled for a few seconds with both thumbs. 'Right, that's done.' She returned the phone to Lucy's handbag.

Lucy had not fully woken up so missed most of what Charlie was saying. 'Lucy darling, please listen to me. Our flight to Kolkata is booked for 3.30 pm tomorrow afternoon. That means we still have one morning together before we have to catch our flight. Lots of time to do things. Did you hear?'

'Yes. I'll be fine. You take care, now. Promise!'

'You're the one who needs to take care. Farm girl!'

Lucy threw her Teddy Bear at Charlie. She ducked, bent down, and picked up the Teddy bear. She held it up to her face, studied it for a few seconds, then gave it back to Lucy. She shook her head.

'Dear, dear Lucy!'

LOSING IT, by Lucy Braithwaite
(Lucy's diary)

As soon as Charlie was out of the room, I found Chimlin's card. I rang the number.

Chimlin replied very quickly. She could meet me that morning. We arranged to meet at a small bar close to my hotel.

I arrived first and found a table by the wall with a view of the street.

I ordered a fruit juice. She arrived a few minutes later. She looked radiant. The oppressive heat didn't seem to bother her.

She asked me what my name was. I hadn't thought about this. Without hesitating, I told her my name was Lucy.

Without further ado, Chimlin told me he wanted to meet me. Did I want to meet him?'

I nodded my head. I asked her what his name was?

She said Nat. That's easy. Nat and Lucy.

I realised I had suddenly revealed myself in a way that I would regret later. What the heck? I would have to be vigilant in future. She sensed my reluctance. To keep the momentum going she ran her fingers through my hair which was down. I turned my face to make it easier for her.

She said I was very beautiful. She paused, waiting for my reaction. I closed my eyes and tried to visualise him.

I saw him standing in his flowing robes. The colour of his skin. His proud bearing. His facial features. There was nothing I wanted more at that moment than to meet him. My expression said it all. Of course I wanted to meet him. That was an understatement. I wanted to do more than meet him. Meeting him was only a beginning. I wanted much more. I felt an enormous sense of relief. The truth was out. My heart was pounding, and I couldn't breathe.

She cupped my chin in her hands and looked at me very intently. Okay. If you don't like him. That's it. All fine. No problem.

She said she would call him. She took out her phone which was bright pink and walked to the door. She made contact. Spoke for a few seconds, nodded her head. Ended the call. She returned smiling.

'All fixed up. I meet you here this afternoon. Three o'clock? Okay?' I nodded.

She leant towards me and gave me a hug. I smelt her perfume. Felt her taut body again. We become accomplices in an act that felt shamelessly wicked and totally outrageous. What would Charlie think? What would my mother think?

My first thought was to find another hotel. If I was going to do this, I needed space. I had to be alone. I needed to collect my thoughts. It was as if I was on drugs, cocaine, or LSD, or magic mushrooms. None of which I had ever tried. Was I being absolutely crazy? I chose a hotel a block away from the first one. It was older and smaller. I took only what was absolutely necessary. I kept my passport and air ticket. I left my camera with the suitcase containing my wedding clothes. I also left a short note to Charlie explaining things as best I could without going into too many details. After some deliberation, I left her with the amulet I had picked up from the floor of the massage parlour. In my befuddled mind I felt it might come in useful.

My new room was smaller, with two single beds close together. It had a shower. I thought of the wedding. My mother. I dashed all thoughts of the wedding out of my mind. This could be the very last chance. Charlie's very own words to me. My very last chance to do what? What was it I was about to do that I had never done before? Live? Express myself? Be myself? So many questions.

What to wear? I put on the new underwear that Charlie had bought me. I was feeling very nervous. I had a shower.

I was at the bar in good time. I ordered a glass of fruit juice. When it came, it was an usual green colour, the likes of which I had never seen before. I asked the waitress what it was? Kiwi fruit she said. I needed to collect my thoughts. Decide if I was being stupid. He was a monk, after all. Surely that meant something?

Chimlin appeared and caught sight of me. She smiled and waved. She had changed. She didn't come in. She waited outside for me.

I finished my drink in one gulp and followed her out. We crossed the road, and Chimlin led me to a pier where a long boat was drawn up. We climbed aboard and Chimlin advised me where to sit to avoid the spray. The water smelt strong. Heavily polluted with sewage. The twin motors surged into life and the bow rose up. Very soon we were whipping along at an amazing speed leaving all other boats behind. We travelled for three stops. Chimlin got up and I followed her. We walked down a narrow street lined with tall trees. A taxi was parked near the curb some distance away. Chimlin waved and it started up and came up to us and stopped. Without saying anything Chimlin opened the back door and we both climbed in. We were off. We drove in silence for twenty minutes, the noise of the airconditioning a deterrent to speech. The road was bumpy, and the driver drove slowly and carefully.

The taxi stopped outside a modern concrete and glass house two stories high with tiled roof. There was a door in the wall and a bell. Chimlin rang the bell. The gate opened a chink, then opened fully.

Chimlin walked in. I followed. The gate was closed and padlocked behind us.

We entered a courtyard with a rectangular pond in the centre with concrete stepping- stones across it. Big fat orange and white koi carp swam languidly under the water lilies. The vibrant colours of hibiscus, poinsettia, frangipani and bougainvillea clashed like a painting by Gauguin. As I walked across the fish came to the surface with their mouths gaping. Orchids in hanging baskets lined one side of the courtyard. Through a wrought-iron gate I glimpsed the turquoise blue of a swimming pool shimmering in the sun. Under a shady hibiscus bush was a wooden bench, a wooden table and two chairs. I could hear running water. Orange and gold-coloured birds chattered excitedly in the tree above us. A round nest suspended from a long twig made from blades of grass shaped like a coconut with a neat entrance was swaying in the wind. A small bird with a black head was fluttering its wings as an inducement to a drab female perched next to him.

She invited me to sit. She pointed to the chairs. I chose one which provided a view of the property. I expected her to sit with me. Instead, she walked purposefully up some steps and made her way towards the house and disappeared through an open door.

She returned with a tray of drinks, a brass bowl of sliced mango, kiwi fruit, and litchis, a jug of fruit juice with ice, a towel and a jade-coloured sarong which was for me to wear.

She asked me if I wanted to swim. I nodded. I was feeling the heat. The new clothes were uncomfortable.

She sat down next to me and pointed to the fruit. There were fruits that I had only ever seen in cookery books. Our greengrocer back home never stocked them. I helped myself to several golden slices of mango oozing with juice. Chimlin took a ripe litchi and put it into her mouth. She punctured a hole in the shell with a tooth and sucked the white flesh away from the pip with a loud slurping sound. White juice ran down her chin. With her glistening teeth and round red tongue she tugged the white flesh away from the brown shiny pip and swallowed.

We were so absorbed with eating we didn't speak. The sun smacked me on the face. I smelt freshly mowed grass and heard birds twittering. The blue sky was washed out. The sun vibrated. When I had eaten and wiped my face Chimlin was waiting. She extended her arm. I took her hand. We passed through the wrought-iron gate. There was a small brick and thatch structure to one side of the pool. It was very hot and humid. A swim would be just what I wanted, but I hadn't brought my swimming costume. I looked around the room to see if I could see one hanging up, but there was nothing. Chimlin quickly realised my dilemma. She showed me where to change. She watched me while I undressed. I put on the sarong. Chimlin was also undressing. She led me to the pool where she stepped into the water. She invited me to join her.

I looked around. There was nobody else in sight. I looked up at the building that loomed over us with it's wall to ceiling plate glass windows curtained and drawn. We appeared to have the whole place to ourselves. I wondered where he was.

I removed the sarong and laid it on a low wall by the pool. Stark naked, I stepped swiftly into the water and crouched down, cradling my breasts with my hands. I gasped. I turned on my stomach and swam towards the deeper end, but Chimlin caught me by the toe of one foot and pulled me back. She put my toes in her mouth and bit them gently. She giggled. I objected, but Chimlin smacked my bottom. I retaliated by splashing her.

The moment was shattered by the sound of a car arriving. I heard angry shouting. A woman's voice arguing. She was shouted at by a young man. A dog barked loudly.

A middle-aged woman appeared. She strode vigorously towards us shaking her head. Her fists were clenched, and her lips were squeezed into a tight ball.

I submerged with just my nose above the water.

She shouted at Chimlin. Chimlin grabbed her sarong from the wall and wrapped it round her hips before climbing out of the pool and walking up to the woman. The woman slapped her face. She then turned to me and talking in accented English, asked,

'Where you from? England? You must leave. Please, get dressed and go home. If you stay, it is very dangerous for you. Believe me!'

I grabbed my sarong and wrapped it around my dripping shoulders. When the lady was not looking, I climbed out of the pool and with as much dignity as I could muster, headed for the changing room, where I quickly changed into my clothes. The woman led me to the gate. 'I'm sorry.' She pushed me out gently. I heard the padlock rattling as she locked the gate behind me.

THEODORA PERFECT

I was upset, aroused, and confused. Drops of water ran down my cheeks and wet my blouse. I stood outside in the dusty street. A gust of wind blew an empty plastic bag across the street. A starving bitch with a hungry litter to feed and pendulous udders sniffed at an overflowing rubbish bin. I looked for a taxi. There were none to be seen. Two crows flew overhead calling raucously. I began to get worried. I had no idea where I was. Round the corner a taxi appeared. It was the same taxi that had brought us. The driver spotted me and drew up beside me. I climbed in. I told him to take me to the boat. At the pier he stopped, and I asked him how much? He shook his head. I bought a ticket for the boat and headed back to my hotel.

I felt annoyed and confused. Jilted. One half of my mind said, stop this madness. This is not you. But it was the other part, the part that was growing in stature which had me in its claws and wouldn't let go. The older woman's warning came back to me. What did she mean? What was dangerous? Who was she? What did she know that I should know?

The nagging doubts returned. He was a monk after all. Surely that spoke for itself. Was this how I wanted it to be? Was he going to be my knight in shining army like in Tennyson's poem? The way I was feeling towards Nat seemed somewhat different.

I ordered food brought to my room. There was a text message from Charlie wanting to know where I was. I told her all was well. I thought of my mother. What was she making of the whole business? I shuddered. Better not to go there.

Very early the following morning I got a call from Chimlin. She wanted to know where I was staying. I told her. She said she was coming up.

I barely had time to hide my nightie and Teddy under the pillow when there was a gentle knocking. I unfastened the door. It was Chimlin. She was alone, and had a broad smile, and looked fresh in a cotton skirt the colour of ripe pomegranates that revealed her knees.

She held me by my shoulders and looked intently into my eyes. She explained that Nat was very, very, sorry for bad woman who shout and make trouble last time.

60

I didn't know what to say. Realising this, she reached into her handbag.

She handed me a small heavy object. It was an ornate bottle of pale gold liquid with a fancy cap that was slightly phallic in shape. I held it up and looked at the label. Heure Exquise by Annick Goutal. Perfume! I knew nothing about perfume.

Chimlin had a puzzled look on her face. She snatched the bottle back and removed the gold stopper. She squirted a tiny drop into her palm and put it under my nose.

I breathed in deeply and closed my eyes. The fragrance was strong. I became overwhelmed with a great many conflicting thoughts and emotions. All I knew was that it was very expensive. That it came from someone who lived in a world where such things played a significant part. That it was assumed I knew about such things and would be impressed. What was I supposed to think? I shook my head, not because I did not appreciate the gift. The perfume was exquisite. It made me feel like somebody I had never been, but had secretly wished to be. I was at a loss.

Chimlin was watching me very closely. My reaction was not what she had expected. She looked hurt. She assumed the perfume was not to my taste. That I preferred another brand.

I shook my head. It was too expensive. Not me at all. She explained that it was very expensive and that this brand was very popular with English people.

I tried to explain. He, I meant Nat, must not waste his money like this. He does not know me. He must save his money. These were the words my mother would have used.

I realised for the first time that I was calling him by name. Giving him a physical entity. That he was not just a figment of my imagination but a living, breathing creature.

Chimlin's mood relaxed when she heard this. She said Nat has many money. This is nothing for him.

With the problem resolved, and just to please Chimlin whom I was now growing fond of, I took the perfume back. I removed the cap and did what Chimlin had done. I sniffed it, closed my eyes. My head swam. I visualised a riverbed reed-clogged at dusk embraced by long shadows, slender irises swayed gently in the reeds by the stream, tiny violets pushed their heads through the damp earth. It reminded me of the painting by Pre-Raphaelite painter William Waterhouse of Ophelia that Charlie had talked about. "In her lap she holds rosemary, pansies, fennel, columbine and daisies."

Tell Nat I love it.

Chimlin shrieked. She hugged me, and I almost dropped the bottle. I started laughing. We couldn't stop. Her mood changed suddenly. Became purposeful. She patted the mattress beside her. She went across the room to where she had put her handbag. Bringing it over she sat beside me.

I was curious. I leant across to see what it was she wanted to show me.

Chimlin removed a small cordless razor. She looked sternly into my face. I felt her determination and was awed by it. She told me that Nat was very particular. He wanted me to look very special for him. She said that in Thailand they had different customs. Different from British. They liked body with no hair. She indicated with her glance that she meant my crotch.

Then I realised. She added that in a Buddhist country this was important. I recalled her shaved body in the parlour. It certainly looked tidier. Maybe from a hygiene point of view in the hot weather. I had never seen the need for this, or even thought of it as something that needed removing. It was a part of me, like the rest of me. I hesitated. She expertly switched the topic.

She said I had very beautiful hair. She wanted to know why I had it tied up all the time? She untied the elastic hair grip and my hair tumbled down around my face. She gazed at me in wonderment, shaking her head. She beckoned. She said she wanted to make me totally irresistible to Nat. Then she said something that brought me to my senses like a slap in the face. She said he loved me so much already. That what she was about to do would make him totally crazy for me.

Let me make you even more beautiful for Nat. He loves you so much already. This will make him totally crazy. Lie on the bed. On your back. That's nice. You ticklish? I think so!

I asked her what she was talking about. He had barely seen me before.

She was taken aback by this. 'Oh yes,' she said. 'He saw you when we swim in the pool. He has, how do you call?' She held up her hands as though she was holding a pair of binoculars.

'Binoculars?'

She nodded. 'He watched us and like you too much!' She burst out laughing. I felt embarrassed. The shaver started buzzing. Chimlin put one hand on my knee and spread my thighs and pushed me onto my back. She tugged my knickers down past my knees and ankles. The shaver felt cold on my warm skin. At first it tickled, and I squirmed. She shooshed me. She started down around my bottom using the fingers of her left hand as a safety barrier. She moved very slowly up along my vulva. Having done one side, she moved over to the other side leaving a strip of hair down the middle of my stomach. When the rest had been done, she worked with concentration on this narrow strip leaving a forked tongue of hair like the branches of a spreading tree that stopped on the bridge of my pubis and stretched about two inches up my stomach.

Admiring her work she stood up. My blonde curls lay in tiny heaps on my stomach and on the bedcover. Satisfied, she bent down and blew the fluff away. She brought over a small mirror from her compact.

I could only nod my head. She couldn't resist it. She bent and placed a small kiss on my crotch now totally exposed and starting to reveal itself.

It tickled. I closed my thighs around her head in a vice-like grip. I started to feel aroused. I grabbed her by the hair and pulled her away.

She pushed me back onto the bed panting slightly and pointed to my toes. Chimlin painted my toenails the colour of ripe cherries. And my fingernails to match. She put all her apparatus in her bag, then headed towards the shower inviting me to follow her.

THEODORA PERFECT

She stripped quickly and entered the shower. There was not much room. I tied my hair in a tight bun.

We soaped one another. I took care not to get my hair wet. I pinched her nipples. She kissed me. I smacked her bottom. We giggled like young girls. Chimlin's phone rang. She leaped out of the shower grabbing a towel on the way splashing water onto the floor and nearly slipping. She spoke for a few seconds, nodded her head, then switched the phone off. Her manner changed instantly.

'Quick, quick, get ready. We must go. He wants you,' she said.

I left the shower and dried myself. Chimlin wrapped a silk scarf around my hair and tied it in a bow at the back. As we were ready to leave the room, she leant forward and sniffed me. I shook my head.

'Come on, Lucy, most important you smell good for Nat. Not so?' She said. 'Where you put the perfume I give you?' she demanded.

I pointed to the dressing table. She leaned over and snatched it up and handed it to me. Watching my movements intently, I opened the perfume. I had never used perfume before, let alone been given it. I dabbed some behind my ears, on my wrists as I had seen my mother doing. Just as I was putting the top back on Chimlin grabbed it and poured a few drops on her index finger, lifted my skirt, and put a dab at the top of each thigh.

She giggled.

We left the hotel. Chimlin walked ahead in the direction of the canal and with me following feeling very otherworldly. We caught a long-tailed boat, much the same as the day before. Chimlin took a large pair of sunglasses from her bag and placed them carefully on my face.

They were wrap-arounds, and I could hardly see a thing. Probably the main objective. The ride lasted longer than before. At one pier we got out and climbed into a much smaller boat. There was less noise. The air was sweeter. I could hear bird song and the lapping sound of water reflected off sun-drenched brick walls. Snatches of conversation were thrown into the warm air from houses we passed. Occasionally I heard the sounds of farm-yard animals: chickens clucking, and pigs grunting.

We stopped and got out. We climbed up steps onto a pavement of sorts. I had trouble seeing where I was going. The surface was uneven. I nearly fell. Chimlin grabbed my hand. We walked for a few minutes and stopped. Chimlin stopped and rang a bell. A gate opened, we entered. She removed my sunglasses. The light dazzled me at first. We were in a garden full of flowering shrubs. Pink and yellow hibiscus, scarlet poinsettia, white frangipani. A large jade-coloured swallowtail butterfly flitted from flower to flower. The grass was neatly mowed and smelt sweet. A hammock suspended from a tree swayed gently. The house was large and sprawling, single-storey and largely made of wood. Orange tea-roses the size of apples sprawled across a flowerbed by the steps. Their perfume was undeniable. I tottered up creaking wooden steps like a drunk onto a wide veranda deep in shade. Hanging baskets overflowing with exotic orchids lined the verandah.

Chimlin led me through a dark living-room with polished wood floor and rattan furniture with curtained windows drawn back to allow whatever breeze there was to enter. A large metal fan hanging from the ceiling rotating laboriously was the only sound to be heard. She told me to sit down. I chose a large rattan chair facing the windows and waited. Birds were calling from the garden. I could hear her doing something in the kitchen. She returned with a jug of fruit juice and two glasses. The stillness and the quiet enabled me to become contemplative. What were my aspirations? What did I really want from all this?

Chimlin's voice broke my thought train. She asked me if I wanted a drink. She poured juice into two glasses and handed one to me.

She left me, glass in hand and went through an open doorway. I heard voices. She came back. 'Do you like dancing?' She walked over to a sound system and turned it on.

It was Chris Rea, the song, Let's Dance. She beckoned to me to join her on the carpet. She smiled and put her arms loosely around my waist. It was too hot for bodily contact. The Heure Exquise was a potent reminder of what was to come. I felt uneasy and anxious.

I asked her what was happening. Where was he?

THEODORA PERFECT

She told me not to worry. She said he was busy. He would come. She said it was very important that we were both ready.

I asked if he could speak English.

She frowned. She said of course he understand English. That he was very educated. No problem with understanding you. He had a university degree. Switzerland.

I felt slightly reassured. However, the look on Chimlin's face gave me another feeling. She seemed to be mocking me.

She put one arm on my shoulder and the other on my waist. I felt hot and sticky. The fan was not doing its job.

She was the leader and I followed. She danced with a natural fluency. Her body taut. She started giggling. A door opened behind us. I smelt incense, and something else.

To distract me she drew me against her so that her stomach rubbed against mine. Our thighs touched. I knew we were being watched. The physical contact allowed the 'new me' to surface. She stopped dancing and beckoned me.

The tone of her voice expressed the new mastery she had over me and I responded as she expected I would. She led me by the hand into a large bedroom which had the curtains drawn. The only light a narrow triangle where the curtains didn't quite meet. There was a double bed with a brass headboard. An oriental painting on the wall. Brass candlesticks. The smell of incense. A slight breeze from the garden caused the heavy curtains to sway gently. The angular shaft of bright sunlight expanded briefly. I smelt mown grass and roses.

She pointed to a low chair and told me to sit down. I obeyed.

She removed my shoes and knelt on the carpet in front of me. She wrapped the scarf which had covered my hair around my eyes and knotted it firmly behind my head. I definitely couldn't see anything. She helped me up and led me the few paces to the bed. A gentle push and I was lying on my back. She took one foot in her hand and blew softly between my toes. It tickled and I squirmed. She did it again more gently and I giggled. She put my big toe in her mouth and sucked. It felt like a kiss. It reminded me of the way she had removed the skin of the litchi in the garden with the swimming pool. She playfully ran her fingers up and down my calf in the way a mother encourages her child to eat its food when it is not in the mood. I was very ticklish, and she knew this. She did it on the other leg. When I couldn't control myself and was on the point of screaming, she changed legs, going higher and higher each time until she was on the smooth skin of one thigh. Just her fingertips. Like tapping on a keyboard. She slid my dress up. Started kissing my thighs. Pushed my thighs open and placed kisses between my thighs. Tugged my knickers off gently. I made no effort to thwart her. I was entirely in her power. She moved around to the head of the bed so that she could catch hold of my wrists, one in each hand, pulling tighter, tighter, pulling me back, elongating my body, stretching my spine.

A floorboard creaked. I heard footsteps. Chimlin tensed. Another set of hands stronger and hotter took one foot in each hand squeezing my toes. I felt soft lips touch the skin under one foot then the other. Fingers ran along the outside of my calves feeling the muscles, repeated several times, each time the strong fingers digging deeper. Chimlin kept up the pressure on my arms restraining me. One at one end, she the other, me in the middle.

Using my feet as handles my legs were pushed to one side to expose my thighs. My buttocks were raised slightly, bending my knees backwards and outwards tilting my hips upwards. I became conscious of the music. I felt myself under scrutiny. Like an item. I imagined Chimlin trying to gauge his reaction to what he saw. I so wanted to please him. That was top of my agenda, to please him. No matter what. I had no capacity to control what was going on and what was going to happen.

What happened next was ordained. Like an arrow hitting the target. I felt a feather-light touch of lips on my crotch. My bullseye. He dragged his moist tongue along the slippery cleft beneath, nursing it creatively and knowingly. Sucking. Fingers entered there.

I had a vision of his noble face in the monastery in devout worship offering himself up wholeheartedly to his deity, every atom of his being directed towards that one goal. I wanted to look into his eyes. I tried to free my hands so that I could remove the scarf and see into his eyes. Chimlin obliged by releasing my hands and pushing my face into her wet crotch. I reached behind and sank my nails into her buttocks. She squealed. I couldn't breathe. She grabbed both my arms and pulled me back with a determination that frightened me.

Something nuzzled in the cleft between my buttocks. I tried to close my thighs to oppose it, but he gripped me tighter and aligned my body just as he wished. I tensed in anticipation. I had no power to resist. I only wanted to please him.

I was on a deserted beach. It was dawn. Pale golden light. Flat sand. Waves gently advancing, receding. In the distance approaching a dark horse at full gallop with flashing eyes. Mane floating wide. The rhythm of the hooves on the hard sand. The waves building, pushing, ever closer, wetting my feet, withdrawing, hooves thundering, their rhythm increasing the noise deafening. A huge wave builds, teeters, crashes down in a flurry of spray which engulfs me, the horse rides over my body crushing me obscuring the sun. Sharp hooves slash my flesh. I cannot breathe. I was drowning and being dragged out to sea. The pull of the tide was remorseless. The stallion diminishes in size then vanishes. Chris Rea's words in the song came through to me.

"My face was burning, my lips on fire."

He groaned, over and over like an animal. Chimlin released my hands and cradled me in her arms, kissing my burning throat, pushing her breasts into my face smothering me.

She removed the scarf. While my eyes adjusted to the light, I raised myself. In the distance caught a flash of muscular shoulders and bronze skin vanishing through a door which was slammed shut.

She told me to get dressed. She picked up my knickers and shoved them into my hand. She pointed down a corridor and said I could use the bathroom. I tried to stand. My legs would not support me. I collapsed onto the bed. Slowly I put my clothes on, adjusted my hair, put my shoes back on. I tried standing again. I made it to bathroom unaided. I sat on the toilet. Afterwards I stood in front of the basin and sloshed water over my face. I couldn't recognise myself in the mirror.

In the living room Chimlin took my hand and lead me back to the sitting-room. She was dressed. She smiled. Kissed me gently on the lips. It was too sudden. I needed to come down slowly, gently. I reached out to her and buried my head in her neck not sure whether to cry out or just weep.

I couldn't look her in the eyes. I needed to change my clothes. I felt wet and sticky. Partly disgusted, partly exultant. Something had definitely changed inside me. Was this how I wanted it? How I had planned it? It wasn't. All I felt was confusion. My emotions had been released like a pack of hunting dogs on the morning of a hunt. I needed more than this. This was just a beginning.

Back at my hotel I removed my knickers, still damp. I stretched out the flimsy fabric and buried my nose in it. It hung limply over my face like a shroud. I closed my eyes breathed deeply. I smelt it. The jungle smell of our bodies fully awakened. A patch of clotted yoghurt. His seed gone to waste. Ever more vividly I could see the horses. I placed the knickers in the box and locked it.

'Exhibit number one, your honour!'

I took out my diary and started writing the first entry of, 'How I lost It.' I texted Charlie to say I was Okay.

I wrote nonstop, and didn't climb into bed until after midnight. I slept soundly, and only woke when I heard the cleaners talking in raised voices as they trundled their wagons along the corridor outside my bedroom. I went down for a leisurely breakfast, and by the time I returned to my room it was nearly midday.

I called my brother. It took an enormous effort. I had been putting it off. Where to begin? How to put into words what I had done. What I was feeling. Did I really know myself? He was ten years older than I was and we had never been very close. He was always driven. Knew from a very early age what he wanted to do, and how to achieve his goals. I realised very early on that he pitied me for not having done anything with my life. Well! Here I was doing just that. I thought of my mother. Oh dear. She must be going demented. I managed to convince him that there was nothing to fear. That I was in control and if things got out of hand there was always Charlie who I could call and seek help. She would know what to do. I never mentioned the wedding and nor did he. I was more concerned about my mother who would surely be having hysterical fits by now.

The next morning Chimlin called me. She was in the foyer. I told her to come up. She was as bouncy as usual with a big smile, wearing a very colourful skirt and white blouse. She had two large parcels under her arm which she put on the bed. She came up to me and kissed me on the lips. Her mouth was soft and wet. Her contact gave me pleasure and reassured me that all was well.

She undressed, tossed her clothes on the bed, and headed for the shower. She turned on the water and while she regulated the temperature, she beckoned to me to join her. I undressed hurriedly unwilling to miss out on the fun. She found my flannel and squirted soap onto it. She began washing me gently.

After our shower we dried and sat naked on the bed. Chimlin opened the first parcel and brought out a pair of the most beautiful shoes I had ever seen. They were black and had long stiletto heels with red underneath. They were elegant and very sexy. I was spellbound.

Chimlin giggled. She said they were made by Christian Louboutin.

I had never heard of Christian Louboutin. I smelt the new leather, felt the soft velvety texture. They were too expensive for me. I looked puzzled and shook my head. To reassure me she told me he had plenty money.

I put one shoe on and tried to stand. I nearly fell over. I sat on the bed and put the other one on. I stood, arms out for balance. They fitted beautifully. I looked at myself in the mirror. I felt something new inside me. Something that frightened me.

In the second parcel were two expensive silk cheongsam dresses. These had a slit up both sides, had a high butterfly collar with sleeves that just covered the shoulders and a skirt that reached below the knee. One was black, the other red, with a floral motif down one hip. She told me to wear the black one. It fitted perfectly. It just covered my knees. It fitted tightly around my hips and bottom. The shoes and the dress went well together. I felt a different person.

Would Charlie recognise me now?

Still she was not satisfied. What was it now? She lifted the dress and pointed to my knickers and made a dismissive motion with her hands. I understood. I slid the dress up my thighs and pulled down my knickers. Chimlin came behind and unzipped me. She peeled the gauzy material down over my shoulder-blades, freed my arms, unhooked my bra, and pushed the straps off my shoulders. With the dress hanging off my shoulders she tugged my bra free revealing my breasts. She couldn't resist. She leant forwards, took a breast in each hand, and squeezed, kissing me on the lips at the same time.

Swivelling me round she tugged the zipper up my back to my neck and her final gesture was to pat me on the bottom. Impatient once again, she headed for the door.

I dabbed perfume, behind my ears, at the base of my neck, my wrists. She was watching. I slipped my hand between my thighs. She giggled.

I could hardly stand and nearly toppled over. She reached out to support me. She said no walking. Taxi. Walking from the lift to the swinging doors of the hotel demanded a great deal of concentration. I felt the eyes of the receptionists watching every step I made. What were they thinking?

The strange feeling I had felt earlier was now very strong. We left the hotel and Chimlin pointed to a modern pink taxi waiting at the curb. We hopped in. She put on my sunglasses.

The drive was a long one. We left the main boulevards and soon were heading away from the hustle and bustle of the centre of town. The taxi stopped. I was still wearing the sunglasses. I put my hand up to remove them, but she stopped me. We entered the foyer of a very modern block of apartments all marble and glass. Chimlin made for the lifts. She pressed the button for the top floor. As the lift lurched upwards, she removed my sunglasses. The lift stopped. The doors opened. We had reached the Penthouse. We walked down a short flight of steps into the living room. One wall was all glass with sliding glass doors that were open. Through the glass I could see the city below us and the main river and all it's canals. It was mind boggling. Three long sofas were drawn into a horseshoe facing the windows. The lighting was invisible, the air-conditioning up high.

Chimlin led me to the sofa facing the window. She dimmed the lights even further, turned on western music. There was incense burning. She fetched a tray with drinks on it. She asked me what I wanted. I had no idea. She suggested an apple martini. It was green and came in a long-stemmed glass with sugar round the lip, and a slice of lemon hanging perilously on the rim. She had the same. She toasted me. I took a big sip. I coughed and spluttered. Chimlin giggled. I had never drunk spirits before.

She told me to take it easy. Not to rush. She used my name. This was the first time she had called me Lucy. At some point she closed the curtains. The room was suddenly dark, lit only by pencil-thin wall lights. I was sitting on the sofa facing the windows. She came over and knelt beside me. My dress fell away revealing my thighs. We began kissing. Chimlin raised her head and looked past me over my shoulder. I turned, and saw him for the first time. He was wearing a mask, the likes of which I had seen revellers at the Venice Carnevale wearing. It was gold and picked out in black with signs of the zodiac. It covered his eyes and reached to the curve of his cheek bones leaving his mouth and chin exposed and his whole forehead. It accentuated his swollen lips and the harsh line of his jaw. My hope of seeing his eyes was dashed once again. He was wearing a long black gown that reached his feet and a crimson sash around his waist. He was bare-footed. The thick carpets muffled his approach.

I had a sudden overpowering feeling that what I was doing was wrong. That I must end it right now or die. I felt real fear for the very first time. I pushed Chimlin away from me and turned, looking for the door, for an escape. Chimlin reached for me grabbing me by my hair and pulled my face into her bosom suffocating me. I pushed her away, but she was very strong. She cried out in a strangled voice that was part fear and part anger.

She repeated my name, over and over again. Don't worry Lucy. I am your friend.

I WAS THE LADY OF SHALOTT

I heard his voice for the first time. He gave Chimlin a command. His voice was deep and assertive. She turned and released me and went to him obediently. I was no longer THE object. At that moment I could have found the door and made my exit, but something held me back. It was the new me again. Stronger than ever. I was fascinated by what would happen next.

He lifted Chimlin effortlessly and carried her to the settee laying her down gently. She encircled his hips with her legs. She knew his body and how to respond to it. I watched fascinated but at the same time jealous. I wanted to be part of this too. I saw it for the first time. It showed itself between the folds of his tunic. It was not what I expected. Unashamed and arrogant. The head broader than the shaft, but flatter like a shovel, a ripe glossy plum bursting with juice. A different colour and texture. Reptilian. Purplish. It bobbed up and down. Primordial and sinister, like an iguana seeking its prey, at the same time very beautiful. Able to see in the dark. Existing only by feel. Evolved purely for pleasure with a purpose all of its own. The pleasure a by-product of creation. Able to give and derive pleasure. This one had worked many women's bodies. Knew its way around.

I saw Chimlin's cell phone lying on a chair. I had a sudden brainwave. They were totally engrossed in each other. I sat on the carpet out of sight. I switched it on. I found the most recent message. Searched for the number. Found it, shared it with my number. My phone pinged. I switched it off. Put Chimlin's phone back. The session was reaching its climax. I waited my moment. His thrusts slowed. He grunted, I grabbed hold of Chimlin's feet and pulled her away. She squealed and reached for me. I pushed her back harder. She resented this and grabbed me. He didn't interfere. He liked being an observer. He was the director, set the scene, chose the actors, and watched.

His eyes were in shadow. I looked into the black holes of the mask and saw his eyes glinting. I felt wet between my breasts and wet between my legs. I needed to put it down there. I reached out to touch it. It inclined itself towards me sensing my need. As my fingers closed around it, it twitched and stiffened. Still wet. I knelt and let it bump against my closed lips, my cheek, my chin, letting its tautness express itself anyhow it wished. I felt its blind weight. When it bumped against the corner of my mouth, I opened my mouth and encircled the head with my lips. I expected it to be cold like a reptile, but it was hot, like a dragon. The skin soft over the hardness. The colour of the head changing like a chameleon. I licked the shiny head, grazed its taut curves with my teeth, ran my tongue into the secret recess. I wanted it all to myself. No more sharing. But above all I wanted to see him. I reached for the mask. He was too engrossed to notice my move. I lifted the ribbon which was tied in a bow at the back of his head over his forehead. Chimlin realised my motive and acted quickly pinning my arms. She pulled me away. He readjusted the ribbon and stood up. Chimlin grabbed a hank of my hair and we struggled. She was stronger than I was. I resisted. She slapped my face once, the second time harder. When I was too tired to resist, I looked to him for support, but he had gone. A door closed. The lock turned.

The following morning early Chimlin called me, but I didn't answer. Later there was a knock on my door but I pretended I was out. She called my name repeatedly, becoming more emotional each time. I ignored her. She pleaded. Implored me to talk to her. Warned me to be careful. She was sobbing by then. Her nails rasping against the door. When she had just about given up, she said, Lucy, Nat very dangerous. You be careful. Understand? Please Lucy! You my friend now.

That word dangerous cropped up again. First the old woman at the house and now Chimlin.

With trembling hands, I called his number. The number rang and rang, but he didn't respond. Instead, I sent him a text message saying who I was. That I want to meet him alone. I waited and waited for a response. Finally, my phone pinged. It was him. He wanted to know where I was staying. I told him. He said he would send a vehicle to the hotel.

I sent Charlie a message to say I was all right.

The vehicle would call for me at 11 am. What was I to do in the meantime? When I was sure Chimlin had left the premises, I left my room and sneaked down the emergency stairway. In the foyer I checked carefully to see that she was not waiting for me. I needed to go shopping and prepare myself. Above all I needed to get away from my hotel so that Chimlin couldn't reach me.

Later, back at my hotel. What would I wear? The red dress? The Louboutin shoes? I decided not to wear underwear. I put the perfume in those special places he liked to visit. I brushed out my hair so that it sparkled.

I was wearing my sunglasses and carrying my new handbag.

Reception called. I walked down to the lobby feeling confident to take on the world. I felt I had worn Louboutin shoes all my life. I could smell the perfume.

The receptionist told me there was a taxi waiting for me outside. She watched me intently as I walked past her. What was going through her mind? I couldn't care less. As I left the hotel, I scanned the parking lot and saw a large expensive car. The driver spotted me and waved. I walked towards him.

The driver did not get out. Instead, he opened the back door from inside. I slid onto the seat and closed the door. My bare skin stuck to the fabric of the hot seat. I caught sight of the driver in his rear-view mirror. He was wearing sunglasses and a base-ball cap turned the wrong way round. His head was shaved. He had a muscular neck. The skin was hairless. The car radio was playing loud Thai music.

We set off. The journey was long. I tried to speak to the driver, but he did not respond. We left the city centre and reached small holdings with banana trees and squat brick buildings. Some were growing rice, with signs of citrus in neat rows. Occasionally a water buffalo up to its knees in paddy fields dragged a plow behind it.

How the taxi driver knew where he was going, I didn't know. What went through my mind was that it would be very hard for anybody else to find this place. That was a worry!

We took a turning onto a narrow farm track. We stopped at two imposing metal gates. There were tall pillars on either side with armorial crests on them. The driver got out and opened the gates. We drove through and he closed the gates behind us. We drove down a long avenue lined with palm trees with their trunks like match sticks. We arrived at some low farm buildings with corrugated iron roofs and parked under a banana tree which had large bunches of green bananas hanging from it. There was no sign of anybody. The driver switched off the engine and got out.

An enormous black dog with a distinctive ridge down it's back galloped round the end of the house, tail up, ears pricked, barking furiously. It approached the vehicle cautiously. It recognised the driver and grinned, wagging its tail vigorously. He patted the dog on the head and as it switched its gaze to me it stiffened and growled threateningly. He gave it a terse command and pointed to the house. It returned to the house obediently.

He beckoned to me to follow. We crossed a sun-scorched driveway slashed by dark shadows and up a short flight of wooden steps through double wooden doors that were open. He showed me into a large living room with walls panelled with wood and doors leading off it on all sides. The floor was polished teak. There were rattan chairs with stuffed cushions and a sofa also rattan. There was not a breath of wind. It was stifling. Golden sunlight entered the room through high windows covered by wooden blinds. He walked to a side table with glasses, a silver pitcher of ice and fruit juices. He turned on a fan and opened some blinds.

When he had my full attention, he slowly peeled off his cap, followed by his sunglasses.

I gasped. It was Nat in person. He nodded and smiled.

He said my name. I saw into his eyes for the very first time. They were large, deep set and very dark. I did not expect this at all. I could only gape. He returned my gaze.

"For now we see through a glass, darkly." (Corinthians chapter one 13:12)

What did I feel? I was utterly confused. I didn't know what to feel. I was far, far, out at sea. I could hear waves crashing on a beach.

Down his forehead he had a ragged scar like a bolt of lightning. His head was shaved so that his golden skin shone. I felt weak at the knees.

At last. I was sweating. I felt wet under my arms and down my back. I wiped a bead of sweat from my throat. He noticed.

There was a silver tray with bottles and glasses and an ice container on a side table. He suggested a drink?'

I pointed to a bottle of gin. He showed me a jug of fresh juice. He said it was litchi juice.

I nodded. He removed an ice cube from the ice bucket and held it over my glass. I nodded.

He repeated the action. I nodded again, and he put three cubes into the tall glass. He added a generous tot of gin and stirred it before handing it to me. He had strong capable arms and long elegant fingers. His thumbs were beautiful. The way I liked them. No sign of hair on his arms or on the backs of his hands. On his right-hand ring finger, he had a large gold signet ring. He poured confidently, handed me the glass and with his hand resting lightly on my elbow guided me to a large sofa. I crossed my legs. He returned to the drinks table and poured himself a drink. He came back and sat directly opposite me. I subconsciously adjusted the hem of my dress so that it covered my thighs.

He said, 'Cheers!'

I raised my glass. Took a sip. The alcohol burned my throat. I took a bigger sip. I felt more confident. I coughed, covered my mouth with my hand. Gulped.

He spoke. 'Lucy, I'm sorry to bring you all this way out here, but it's best that we can be together without being disturbed. You agree? This is what you want, isn't it, or am I mistaken? I hope I haven't misjudged you in anyway.' He spoke with scarcely any trace of accent, much like a cultured Indian cricket commentator. His speech was measured, and his words carefully chosen.

I shook my head. I thought of my mother.

Again, the sound of my name. It created a false state of intimacy where none had existed before. His voice was silky and deep. I needed time to gather my thoughts. He was wearing a pale blue silk blouse with short sleeves that reached to his knees, a stiff mandarin collar and a broad sash around the waist and baggy terracotta-coloured pantaloons.

THEODORA PERFECT

The buttons of his blouse were undone, and I could see his muscular chest. He was bare-footed. His toes were as elegant as his fingers with neatly trimmed nails. The feet of a gymnast. He was studying me very carefully. It was the first time he had seen me in daylight. Face to face. I changed the cross of my legs. This time I did not adjust the slit. I parted my knees for just a second then closed them. I thought of Sharon Stone in the movie Basic Instinct. He watched every move I made like a hawk. He shifted his position slightly. He seemed uncomfortable.

He patted the cushion next to him. I walked over and sat beside him, angling my body towards him. I crossed my legs. I smelt his deodorant. He had a broad smile on his face. I was able to see into his eyes again. I needed to find something there which I could connect with, so that I could make sense of what I was doing.

He took my hand and placed it on his knee. He said I was very beautiful. Did I know that?

I nodded and thanked him. He said I was the most beautiful woman he had ever met. To emphasise the point, he squeezed my hand and raised it to his lips. He kissed the back of my hand. Kept it there. I felt his warm breath on my knuckles. He ran the back of my hand along the edge of his jaw until it came to rest against his throat. I released his hold of my hand and explored his throat with my fingers. I leant over and took an ear lobe in my mouth. Sucked it gently. My nose rubbed against his cheek. With my hand I turned his face to face me and with my other hand I cradled his jaws in my hands and looked into his eyes again. I could not gauge his feelings or look into his soul. I leant over and kissed him full on the lips.

He put one hand on my neck. It remained there for a moment then moved down following the hem of my collar until it rested in the space between my breasts.

I felt very vulnerable. I regretted not wearing underwear. He put his hand on my thigh, on the bare skin exposed by the slit which was open. His hand was hot.

From somewhere in the ether a phone rang. The sound broke the magic.

He left my side and grabbed his phone. I recognised the voice. It was Chimlin. He shouted at her in Thai, slapped the phone down and came back. He sat down beside me and reached out to take my hand.

I thought of Charlie. I needed to call her. Tell her where I was. What was going on.

The atmosphere in the room was stifling. I wanted out of the building. This was not how I had visualised it. On the floor was a large crimson prayer mat with a gold border and motif of mauve irises. I bent down to pick it up.

I said, 'Nat, come! Let's go into the garden. It's too hot here.'

With the mat under my arm, I took Nat by the hand and pulled him towards a door leading out to the garden. The sun was dazzling. I shaded my eyes to see properly. At the bottom of the garden was an area in deep shade with grass, surrounded by a high hedge on three sides. Bamboo formed the third side. I staggered down a flight of wooden steps. The dog bounding along beside us was very excited. There was an opening in the hedge. We had to bend down to enter. We disturbed a flock of parakeets that fluttered off screeching loudly. The sky was overcast. I headed for an area of deepest shade where the grass was neatly cut forming a natural carpet. It was very peaceful and private.

The house was invisible. We were near a river or canal. I could hear the sound of water lapping and water birds. I smelled mud. I laid the mat down on the grass. Nat was watching me. I beckoned him to join me. I removed my shoes and placed them neatly beside the mat. I squatted down on the mat leaving space for Nat beside me. He joined me. The dog too wanted to join us on the mat, but Nat gave him a command and he went and lay down by the tree trunk watching us intently.

I sat legs bent, my white English knees gleaming. He sat beside me; we were head-to-head. He was slightly taller than I was. There was a small smile on his lips which were slightly apart. His eyes were burning intensely. I put my hand on his hairless chest and gently pushed him down so that he was lying on his back with hips angled slightly towards me. I leant over him and ran one hand across his forehead, felt the scar that ran between his eyebrows, stroked his cheek, squeezed one ear lobe, felt the sharp contours of his cheek bones down to the corner of his mouth, to his chin. I ran my index finger along his bottom lip, felt the concentrated pressure beneath the surface. He grew impatient and reached for me, but I pushed him back. I leant forward and dropped a kiss on his mouth, like a butterfly alighting on a flower, he wanted more but I pushed him down again. I took his hand and placed it on my throat. I arched my neck. His fingers navigated the contours of my chin, the corner of my mouth. He put one finger in my mouth. I nibbled it gently. Sucked the tip. Tasted him. I grasped his wrist and put his hand where the skin was exposed below my ivory collar bones. His hand felt hot against my skin. It slipped easily under the fabric, reached the outer edge of my breast, moved down over the ripeness, pushing my breast up, squeezing the nipple, drawing it out. It found my other breast. My nipples were hard, exultant, yearning. My breathing accelerated.

I felt constrained by my dress. I sat up and caught hold of the material with both hands and tugged. I struggled to get it past my hips. He assisted. I reached back and pulled it over my head and chucked it on the grass. I felt the cool air on my pale skin. I leant across and straddled him carefully, taking care to sit forward of his groin. He grasped me above my hips with both hands steadying me and raised his hips to meet me. Our bodies collided. I kissed him on the lips, not dwelling long, his mouth wet. I felt his tongue. Something prodded my exposed buttocks. The reptile requested my attention. I reached back freeing it from the constraining fabric of his pantaloons, allowing it to sniff out and fulfil its own destiny. I grasped it by the throat. Felt how hard it was. The skin stretched tight. The head engorged, swollen, hungry, fit to burst, urgently needing to bury itself in the dark of my wet space.

I cupped his chin in my hands and placed a kiss on his lips. This time I pushed down harder and felt his lips respond, felt his tongue again. I allowed my tongue to enter and make contact with his. Our tongues collided and meshed.

He cupped both my breasts and squeezed them. He felt their

roundness, their firmness. His thumbs caressed my taut nipples. I freed them from his hot hands and dragged one taut nipple across his lips from side to side. He tried to bite me. I slapped his cheek. I felt wet between my legs. The reptile would not be denied. I was ready for it. I guided its head towards the wetness and sank down onto it, adjusting the angle so that it went deeper. He arched his back and thrust upward. The reptile felt my warmth and grew in size. I squeezed it to thwart it. In response, his thrusts which began gently, very quickly became rapid and purposeful. His balls in their tight parcel slapped against my buttocks. My breathing adjusted itself to the rhythm of his thrusts and became loud. My chin rested on his forehead. I closed my eyes.

The sun glinted on the furling waves which scurried to the shore still in shadow. The hooves of my stallion thudded on the compacted sand sending tremors through my whole body. His mane flying free tickled my cheek. I was in control, he was mine, perfectly aligned perfectly balanced, moving as one creature formed by nature. The sun broke through the clouds sending long rays that lit up the sand, illuminated the white crests of the waves frothing on the sand. I held my breath, staggered, caught on the edge of eternity, I collapsed onto his chest. He drew me to him in supplication. I cried out. It was too perfect. I was exultant.

In the distance I heard a car, and a woman's voice shouting. I could just make out Charlie's voice calling my name. The dog barked furiously, before bounding away.

I closed my ears. Heard my blood drumming in my head. I breathed again. Gathered my wits. Took in where I was. Looked for my dress. Grabbed it. Drew it over my shoulders pulling it down over my hips and thighs. Nat was already up. I smiled, reached out to hold his hand, to thank him, but he pushed me down. He undid the sash he wore round his waist and tied my hands behind my back. He lifted me up and carried me like a sack of potatoes towards the water. I heard birds calling urgently.

The sprawling branches scratched my thighs. We reached a riverbank. I smelt mud and damp vegetation. I thought he was going to drown me. I struggled even harder, but he was so much stronger than I was. We staggered along the slippery bank until we reached an old houseboat with peeling paint which tied to the bank by a rope which is attached to a metal post. With one hand he tugged vigorously on the rope so that the boat came close to the bank. He dropped me onto the deck and jumped in. He opened the door to the cabin, returned to pick me up and carried me through the door bumping my head in the process. Inside were two bunks separated by a narrow table. He dropped me onto a bunk, tied my feet with a length of rope and retreated locking the door behind him. I tried to scream, but to no avail.

It was unbearably hot. I struggled to breathe. The boat leaned to one side. None of the windows were open. I was sweating. I smelt my body. The boat smelt of fish. I desperately needed a drink. Flies tapped against the closed windowpanes. One landed on my face. I shook my head, but I couldn't dislodge it.

Closer I heard somebody calling. It was Chimlin. The dog barked again, much closer. I heard Charlie's voice calling again hysterically. I tried calling. The boat rocked. I heard footsteps on the deck. The door was forced open. I began sobbing uncontrollably.

I was the Lady of Shalott

LATER BACK IN ENGLAND

Charlie and Lucy meet for dinner at a Chinese restaurant in the village. Afterwards Lucy invites Charlie back to the farm to spend the night. Lucy's mother has moved into a retirement home with her sister. Lucy has the whole house to herself. The house has been decorated in bright colours with silk cushions and oriental fabrics. There are new Arthurian paintings and prints on the walls.

Lucy sat in front of her mirror in what was the master bedroom, the room her parents had slept in for many, many years. She decides to wear a dark green skirt that covers her knees, and an amber-coloured blouse with long sleeves buttoned down the middle held in place by a broad leather belt with large brass buckle. The buckle is a tiger's head with gaping jaws that she hopes Charlie will approve of. Would it resonate with her muladhara chakra, she wondered? The thought makes her smile. To demonstrate the 'new Lucy,' she unfastens the top three buttons of her blouse revealing her cleavage. This sends a little shiver through her body. Her trainers have been banned from the room and now share space next to her Wellington boots by the front door. Instead, she wears claret-coloured velvet loafers embroidered along the side with edelweiss flowers.

She allows her hair to hang in loose shiny coils that cascade over her shoulders, puts just a suggestion of lipstick on her lips. Her fingernails and toenails are painted in a manner Chimlin would have approved of. She decides to wear a turquoise necklace that matches her earrings that she had bought to give her sister-in-law as a wedding present. Behind each ear she dabs a drop of Heure Exquise. She wonders whether to pop a drop elsewhere, but decides against it. No need to waste the precious stuff!

Lucy leads Charlie to the study which is more private and cosier. A fire is burning. Against the wall is a dog basket. She shuts the door. A few rubber toys are on the carpet.

'Charlie. What about a glass of wine?'

'Why not! We've a lot to celebrate!'

'We sure do.' Lucy returns from the kitchen with a bottle of wine and two crystal glasses. She removes the cork with a flourish and pours good measures into each glass.

Charlie settles into a small sofa. Lucy sits opposite Charlie in a chair with her feet folded up under her.

A young black and white puppy appears from nowhere wagging his tail furiously and grinning, displaying a mouth full of sharp young teeth.

'This is Angus, Owen's dog Jess is getting a bit lame so he's supposed to provide support.'

Charlie picks up the puppy which licks Charlie's throat, then lathers her face with his long pink tongue. Charlie wipes her face with the back of her hand and, grasping the wriggling puppy firmly on her lap with one hand, takes a sip of her wine.

'Cheers!'

'Cheers! Nice wine. Certainly not chateau plonk this one.'

'I found my Dad had a stash of lovely wine hidden away in the basement. My mother hardly knew it existed so there it is to be drunk and enjoyed.'

'That I heartedly approve of. To your beloved Dad who I was so fond of.'

'To Dad!'

'Lucy, your hair looks absolutely stunning! You should always wear it down like that. Such a pity to have it bunched up in that dreadful cap all day long. You are a very beautiful girl. Has anybody told you that?'

Lucy didn't reply. She pulls a hank of hair down over her eyes and studied her split ends momentarily.

'Okay, enough of that then. Before you tell me your story, naughty girl, let me tell you what happened when I discovered that you had gone off with Sir Lancelot.'

Charlie released Angus and he bounded off towards Lucy who tickled him under the chin. In the process he nipped her. 'Ow that hurts! He has teeth like needles. Go to your basket.' Angus slunk off to his basket and lay down.

Charlie continued. 'When I read your note I was seized with panic on a monumental scale. Here we were in a foreign country, in a city of millions, known for its quirky customs and attitudes, and it is I who had encouraged you, much against your better instincts to abandon the safety of your country idyll and come here, and what happens? At the very first opportunity you escape from the safety of my arms and go off with, who knows what sort of a guy? Abandoning your brother, the wedding, your family, your mother, the whole bang shoot? It was like being hit by a tsunami. One minute I was standing, the next minute I was on my back engulfed by a towering wave. What was I to do? I had to leave the hotel by ten. I couldn't afford to stay on. I tried calling you.'

'Oh Charlie, I know. I felt dreadful. Believe me. Really dreadful. I thought of you every inch of the way. The wedding hardly entered my mind. I just knew you could cope. Your words kept going through my mind.'

'My God, what words were they? You're blaming me now, are you? I talk such nonsense most of the time.'

'Don't you remember? You likened my state of life to the Lady of Shalott who goes out in her boat because the full meaning of a spell has just dawned on her. She's about to die. You went on about how much of life I was missing. What I had to do to make amends. Remember? All those missed bonks!'

'Ah yes! Now I remember. I won't ask you by how much you have reduced the total.'

Lucy changed the cross of her legs and took a big swig from her glass. She closed her eyes and sighed.

Charlie continued. 'After I booked out of our hotel. I went through all the items you'd left me. I saw the amulet. I called Boribun, my journalist friend, to see if he could put me up for a few nights. I met Boribun for lunch and he took me to his apartment where he offered me his spare room. He's always fancied me. I thought, well, why not! Boribun is Thai but educated in England with a degree in journalism from Exeter University. He said NO to going to the police. Not yet. You were still sending me text messages which meant you were alive and well. He's a crime reporter. We discussed the whole problem. I showed him the amulet. He knew immediately that it belonged to a member of the Thai royal family. That was a start. I needed to phone your brother. I couldn't get hold of your mother, so I managed to reach your farm manager, Owen. Nice chap. He got your brother's number in Kolkata. I told him everything. That it was very unlikely we would make the wedding. That you were missing but, safe. He said he could contact the local British Council offices if you failed to turn up. I told him to wait a bit.' Charlie took a long sip of her wine, wiped her mouth with the back of her hand.

Angus found a piece of rolled up paper and began batting it about on the carpet.

Charlie continued. 'We studied the genealogy of the Thai Royal Family looking for any black sheep. Every royal family has one or two. Just look at the British Royal family. Narong seemed the obvious candidate. Narong's father was a diplomat with royal connections who met Sunanda at university in Switzerland where they were both students. Sunanda is also well connected. He also unearthed the background story on Chimlin. Her name came up when Narong was arrested. Because she was underage, she was let off.'

'Arrested? I can't believe it. What on earth had he done?'

'He raped a young British back-packer, strangled her and pushed her down a cliff into a ravine! He's got a long history of preying on young vulnerable white girls who were out seeking adventure. He used Chimlin as his procurer. She was ideally placed working in the massage parlour. She knew the sort of girls he liked. Usually, these liaisons were short-lived and nothing serious happened. In your case he came up against a very different protagonist and it pushed him beyond his normal limits and also most important, put you beyond Chimlin's protection. Chimlin too realised that you were a different kettle of fish.

'God! How awful!'

'It was obvious that Chimlin was in love with Narong. She realised the only way she could keep him was to pander to his tastes. She was able to regulate his excesses so that they did not spill over and cause anybody harm or get him stuck in prison. I told Boribun what we had done from the time we had arrived in Bangkok to the time you booked out of the hotel. We went through each event. What you had seen on your day alone. The man at the massage parlour who recognised you. Your embarrassment after the massage. I went back to the massage parlour and asked to see the boss lady. I had the amulet with me. I wanted to find out who the young man was. I also wanted to find out who the girl was. I pretended I'd picked up the amulet by mistake and needed to give it back. I found out the girl who had massaged you was called Chimlin. She was not there on that day. She only works three days a week. You left your camera with me. Boribun and I went through all your photos and found the shot of the interior of the Monastery. Even though the light was poor, and it was pretty wide angle we could make out what it was that interested you. That gave us a motive for the photo. We showed it to the Head Lama at the Monastery. From where he was sitting, he was able to get the name of the monk. We printed it out and made several copies. The monastery had Sunanda, Narong's mother's contact details. I called her and we arranged to meet. She was very upset when she heard what had happened. She remembered a young foreign girl arriving at her house. I described you. She said she'd warned you.'

Lucy nodded. 'Yes, poor woman. I was taken to this house. Must have been hers, I suppose. I was in an absolute state of oblivion at the time. It was not me. Somebody else.'

'Yes Lucy. I can just picture it. I arranged to meet her at a quiet cafe in a park. She came across as a very educated person who only wanted the best for you and her wayward son. She was adamant about keeping the whole matter under wraps. She even had a document from her lawyer which we had to sign in which both of us swore to keep silent. Boribun who is not easily intimidated, said it was in our best interests to sign or we could get into trouble with the police. If word reached the monastery, or the police, her son would have to go to prison as this was his last chance to reform.'

'Charlie I am so sorry you went through all that.'

'Didn't Chimlin phone you at any time?'

'Yes, she did, but I didn't answer her calls.'

'Why not?'

'It's hard to explain.'

'All righty. Where were we? Chimlin must have realised when you didn't answer her calls that things were entering a very dangerous phase. She decided to phone Sunanda. Which was very brave of her, because Sunanda has many powerful friends. They're not on very friendly terms, as you realised.'

'I know.' Lucy recalled the angry scene in the garden when she and Chimlin were swimming.

'Thats right. Chimlin did phone when I was with Nat, I mean Narong, on that farm. She probably wanted to know where I was. They spoke in Thai. He took the call and got very angry. That was when I started feeling out of my depth. Had you not found me, I don't think I could have survived much longer in that boat. Like being in an oven. I was suffocating and had almost given up all hope. It was such a remote location. How on earth did you find me?'

'Lucy, do you remember me setting your phone so that it could be traced if you lost it using the Find My Phone app? I switched it on, and it showed us where you were. I showed your location to Chimlin, and she knew immediately where you were. She said she could take me there. I thought it a good idea if Boribun came along too. He would provide a bit of muscle if things got out of hand. We arrived at that farmhouse. Chimlin had been there many times. We searched everywhere for you with no success. We were about to give up when this huge dog appears with a shoe in its mouth. A very elegant black shoe with stiletto heels and red underneath. Chimlin spotted it and knew immediately that you were around somewhere. After that it was just a matter of time. The dog knew where you were. He led us to the boat.'

'I'm so grateful to you and that hound. He looked like a Ridgeback?'

'Yes he was. A Thai Ridgeback. To change the subject. I have something for you Lucy.'

'What is it? Not a Hitachi?'

Charlie burst out laughing and nearly spilled her drink.

'No. Have a look.'

Lucy unwrapped a large package neatly wrapped in brown paper and string. In it was a pair of black shoes with stiletto heels.

'Oh my goodness!' Lucy blushed, held them up for scrutiny. She then put them back in their wrapper and hid the parcel under one of the cushions.

'Christian Louboutin, no less. Excellent taste, I might add. One has tooth marks on it, I'm afraid. Now that you can be frank with me about the experience. Was it all worth it? What have you learned?'

'I won't answer that. Let me show YOU something.'

Lucy went out of the room to return a few minutes later with a small box. Charlie played with the puppy.

'Aha, the little casket.'

'The answers to all your questions lie in here.'

'Show me! I can't wait. Oh my goodness, Lucy you naughty, naughty thing.'

Charlie took a good swig from her glass, put the glass down and held the little box covered with white silk reverently on her lap. She tried to open the lid, but it wouldn't budge.

'It won't open! It's locked!'

Lucy removed a red ribbon from around her neck and gave it to Charlie. On it was a small key. 'Here you are. You unlock it.'

'Oh Lucy, this is such a big moment. Get your phone and take a photo.'

Charlie gingerly inserted the key and opened the lid. Inside, cushioned in red velvet was a book. Charlie took it out.

'Losing It, by Lucy Braithwaite.'

Charlie got up and hugged Lucy. 'You clever girl. Your masterpiece. Well done. Wow, you smell nice, Lucy. What is it?'

'Just a touch of Heure Exquise, that's all!'

'Exquise me!' Charlie burst out laughing. Lucy squealed. The two girls remained in each other's arms rocking from side-to-side shrieking. Angus, also moved by the moment, sat up in his basket and started barking.

'Lucy, here is something you should put into that little casket of yours to be revealed at the chosen moment. Only you will know when that is.'

Charlie took a small beautifully carved amulet from her handbag and placed it reverently in the open mouth of the little casket. She closed the lid and locked it, giving the key back to Lucy.

'You know what it is!'

Lucy nodded, closed her eyes, and took a deep breath. The black stallion was thundering down the beach towards her, it soared over her head and disappeared into the distance. The only sound was Angus scratching himself.

Charlie reverently tucked Losing It into her handbag and smiled. 'I will enjoy reading this, farm girl!'

.

www.ingramcontent.com/pod-product-compliance
Lightning Source LLC
Chambersburg PA
CBHW060944120626
46557CB00003B/1142